Best of 2025
Volume Two

WELL READ Magazine

Edited by Mandy Haynes

WELL READ Magazine's BEST OF Volume Two

Published by three dogs write press

Cover art by Malcolm Glass

Cover & Interior Design by Mandy Haynes

979-8-9898952-7-4 (paperback)

979-8-9898952-9-8 (e-book)

For everyone with a story to share and to the readers waiting to read them.

TABLE OF CONTENTS

Introduction

In January of 2023, *WELL READ Magazine* began accepting submissions for prose, poetry, and visual art. I was blown away by all of the talented poets, authors, and artists that first year and that feeling of excitement I get when reading a new submission hasn't changed a bit in the last three years. If anything, it's gotten stronger. I can't explain how good it feels to share them with readers every month through the online journal, and how much I look forward to publishing the annual anthologies.

Because the submissions are too good not to share again—in print—to give readers another chance to find them. There are no prompts or themes for the submissions so I never know what I'm getting into until I dive in. Every submission is a surprise and each one hits you in a different way. I love that rollercoaster ride feeling with each new entry, so I've broken the traditional rules for publishing collections and kept the anthologies in the same format as what you find in the online journal. You never know what's coming next so get ready for a fun ride!

In the *Best of 2025 Volume Two*, you'll find forty-three submissions written by a fantastic mix of award-winning authors and poets plus new ones to the scene. One submissions in this volume was nominated for a Pushcart Prize: *Burtrell's Pieces* by Jeff Clemmons. The cover art is a photograph by artist, Malcolm Glass, who had several pieces published in October of 2024. You can find that issue and all past issues here www.issuu.com/wellreadmagazine.

If you have a story, essay, poem, or artwork you would like to submit for consideration in upcoming issues of *WELL READ*

Magazine, I would love to hear from you. Visit the website and find the submission guidelines under the Call for Submissions tab in the menu.

As always - thanks for reading!

Mandy Haynes
Editor-in-Chief of *WELL READ Magazine*

Never Give Up

Janet Clare

When my first novel was published seven years ago, the writer and literary critic, John Freeman, suggested I write an essay about publishing a book as an "older" writer. Beyond my desire not to be categorized—not by age, and/or gender, and/or anything at all other than a still-breathing writer—I wrote an essay and positioned myself, not as a debutante, but as someone nevertheless making my debut.

As we all know, the passage of time is relentless. Whether the years are filled with sublime happiness or utter sadness, or, like most of us, with a combination of both. It just goes, and sometimes, our dreams go with it. We turn around and ten or twenty years have whipped by and we are left to wonder what else we could have, should have, done.

As a lifelong reader, I admired writers above all and I'd always wanted to write. But it seemed there was never the time or the space or the confidence to begin. Plus, I'd been married to a writer, which works for some, but not for me; not enough air and patience for two of us. Then everything changed. Divorce, business shuttered, remarriage. Though well past forty, I finally sat down to write nearly every day. At first, it was a kind of journal, which today might be called a blog, but after a year I decided it needed to have form, to tell a story, and I started a novel. I had no idea what a difficult goal I'd set for myself, didn't know enough not to do it. So I kept writing until I found the heart of the story that later would become my first novel.

A year into it, I got sick. The kind of sick that alters your day-to-day existence and threatens your life. However, I was one of the lucky ones, (nearly twenty-eight years later, here I am), and more than anything, once I got through to the other side, I just wanted to finish my book. I kept writing for another year until I had what I thought of as a first draft. But the real turning point came when I happened into an extension class at UCLA with the best of all possible teachers—someone who became a mentor, a guide. It's likely I wasn't always the oldest person in his class, although sometimes, I might have been. But it didn't matter, and I didn't care. I rarely divulged personal information, wanting to be as anonymous as possible to avoid any preconceptions. I threw out everything I'd written and started over, changing the POV from third person to first. Writing, as every writer knows, is rewriting. Fortunately, I had fallen in love with the process. I was hooked, and years later, after my mentor's sudden and devastating death, I kept at it. I thought I couldn't write without him somewhere in my life, but I discovered I could. He was that good, his wisdom had become a part of me. I couldn't *not* write. After a few more years and multiple drafts, I had a finished manuscript to send out, and, amazingly, I found an agent in New York. I thought my troubles were over. I was wrong. The agent did nothing, and I was beyond discouraged. After holding on far too long, I realized the wrong agent might as well be no agent, so I fired her and worked on a new book, although in the back of my mind I kept returning to my Australian story.

Yes, Australia. As an American born in New York and raised in California, I'd always been intrigued by the most far-away places. Australia, Botswana, Patagonia, and I'd been fortunate to travel to some of them. A number of years ago, I was told the true story of a man from Australia who, having spent most of his life in the United States, returned home for his father's funeral only to find that he had a whole other family living on the other side of the country. It is, of course, a big country. But it got me thinking about families and secrets, and all the spaces where we can hide ourselves in a vast and solitary land, the distance between us not always measured in miles. I realized, too, that whenever I'd traveled to remote places, especially outside of cities, it was usually the sky and the air that made the greatest impact on me. And so, I was drawn to the openness of the Australian outback, particularly to the old stock routes where cattle once ran. My interest grew as I learned how these routes were established—by explorers on camels, with wells dug a days' drive apart—and decided to set my story along the famous Canning Stock Route that runs from Halls Creek in the Kimberley of Western Australia to Wiluna in the midwest. Crossing both the Gibson and Great Sandy deserts, 1,900 kilometers through some of the most isolated wilderness on the planet, the Canning is still considered the roughest outback track in the country. In thinking about my story, I wondered what it would be like for an American woman, a New Yorker, to find herself out of her element in a place she never expected to be.

In the early days of my research for the book, I connected with the flying doctors, those magnificent aeromedical professionals who offer emergency and primary health care to remote areas, and I was in touch with them when they rescued the famous art critic, Robert Hughes, after a near-fatal accident while filming in the way outback. "Yup, that was me," my guy said, after swooping in and picking up the crew. "Notice we didn't get any credit." And it was true, news reports rarely referred to the flying doctors, unsung, everyday heroes. I had conjured up a fictitious doctor in an early version of my novel, but he got lost in the dust of later drafts. It happens.

I read everything I could about Australia, visited museums, discovered the deadliest of snakes, the oddest of animals, a multitude of flora, and virtually stalked bikers from the Netherlands as they attempted the Canning Track. All the while, I listened to the beat of the great dead heart of the desert. What I discovered about research was to do it and forget it. Simply let everything you've learned become a part of you so that it seeps into your story. It certainly did for me, and, frankly, has never really left.

After parting with my original agent, I made a number of attempts to connect with the right person, until I finally gave up. But I still believed in my story. Meanwhile, I worked on two other books. Finally, encouraged by the wonderful writing of an Australian friend, and still obsessed by the country itself, I pulled out my manuscript, looked it over, did a bit of sprucing up, and sent it off to a small Australian publisher. They loved it. I was thrilled. For an American writer to find a publisher in Australia, where my heart had traveled for so long, was perfect. My publisher didn't change anything from the original story.

So hardly a debutante in life, I made my debut. It had been quite a while getting there, and like most books, it went through many changes, as did I. But I truly believe in the power of never giving up, and I like to think it took just as long as it was supposed to. I write to be read, and hopefully my story has found an audience. And now, miraculously, I'm making what I like to think of as another debut with my second novel. But the most important thing I've learned, beyond the extraordinary joy of writing, was to never stop, to always make time to do what you love most, and above all, power on.

Lady Sings the Blues

Mike Ross

"Good evening, GOOD EVENING, LADIES AND GENTLEMEN!!" A woman's voice rises above the crowd. "Welcome, welcome! I'm Lilly and I'm so glad to see you all! Sit back, relax with a whiskey and cigarette and let me entertain you." The voice is practiced, professional, the delivery precise and measured. She has done this hundreds of times. The glare of the lights dances off glass and polished wood. Every head is turned toward her as she commands attention.

"I'd like to start with a request from the audience. Would someone like something special?" I hear nothing, as if the crowd is too mesmerized to speak. "Yes… yes… of course I know it, sweety!" she smiles at someone near the front. "Band… that's it… that's the number." After a few seconds, a dark, rich-as-coffee voice floats over us, surrounding the crowd. A few of them have bottles of whiskey, others, cartons of cigarettes, serious partiers. Lilly looks up at the lights, one hand high, her eyes closed and she starts a Billie Holiday jazz favorite, Stormy Weather. The cabaret song envelopes us and the crowd watches silently as she croons.

Don't know why, there's no sun up in the sky, Stormy Weather . . . .

The low, smoky voice resonates like mahogany. With her eyes closed, belting out this classic, Lilly is in a world of her own, cocooned, warm, a place she knows well.

No one stirs, no one raises a hand to order a drink. The voice dominates us, smoothly professional. Like musical magic, Lilly transports her audience, as she warbles her lament about her lost lover. We are lost in her, transfixed, in the moment. It's easy to imagine we're in a smoky cabaret in Berlin or New York and not here.

She sings the last baleful lines,

"Since my man and I ……ain't together, keeps raining all of the time," low and throaty, and finishes with head bowed.

"Thank you, thank you all. You're a wonderful audience." With both hands she throws the crowd a kiss. The place is silent. A few people set down packages and clap a bit, nervously, then a few more join in, until everyone is applauding in a crescending din. Someone yells for an encore.

A disturbance just out of eyesight gets my attention. Thumps and crashes follow the men as they push their way through the throng toward the lady, suitcases and bags tumbling, they bustle toward the performer, the reality of security guys breaking the spell. Lilly hears them, too, and shields her eyes against the blazing lights to see them.

Her face contorts from sublime to confused, frowning first, then changing to fear as she looks around at the displays of stacked cartons of cigarettes, the rows of liquor bottles and the perfume counters in the Duty Free Shop in Frankfurt Airport. She begins tugging at her left ear lobe like a life rope as the men approach. No longer in the cabaret of her mind, she's thrust out of her warm, comfortable world and back into the reality of the airport. The fear is frozen in her eyes.

Someone near her offers her a hand and she steps down off the Canadian Club crate she's using as a stage. A store employee retrieves the candy cone that was her microphone but her other hand still holds an imaginary cigarette. She tugs at the earlobe, making it red raw.

"What is your name please, madame?" a young man asks her in clipped German. She looks at him stupidly. I step forward to translate. The throng that had surrounded her has gone back to shopping, pushing tiny grocery store carts filled with anything but groceries.

"Lilly, the men are asking for your name? Are you Lilly?" I ask her.

She turns to me. "Oh no dear! Tell them my stage name is Lilly. My real name…" But she trails off. On her bag is a name tag. Mildred Hawkins. I read her name in disbelief. She is one of the passengers I'm waiting for at Frankfurt Airport; she's scheduled to be on my next tour.

I tell the security men her name and that she's with me, that I am the guide for her tour. They seem skeptical. I show them my credentials but they linger a moment. Throughout this, Lilly is fixated on a ten foot high display of Ritter Chocolate, having forgotten about the men.

"I'll take care of her," I tell them, but I haven't a clue what I can do. They nod and move off after I assure them she will not sing again. Too bad, I think, this place could use a bit of livening up.

"Lilly… uh, Mildred, where is your husband, Lloyd?" I ask her. Lloyd had been the one to make their reservations with me. About three months ago we'd finalized the trip details and agreed to meet at the Frankfurt Airport. I'd not spoken to him since. Mildred looks like she hasn't heard me so I repeat the question. She gazes around the arrivals hall.

"He must be in the men's room. He must be," she says. She notices the Duty Free Shop and the crate of Canadian Club and blinks. "Where am I?" In careful words, I tell her where she is.

She turns to me and smiles, "Hello. And who might you be?" I say again who I am and suggest we look for Lloyd. "Lloyd?" she says, as if she has never heard the name.

"Your husband," I say.

“Lloyd? Where is Lloyd?” she asks. “Is he here? Oh, my, I want some of that chocolate!” Mildred points at the Ritter Sport display in the shop and takes a step toward it.

“Mildred,” I say as I take her elbow. “Please sit over here and I’ll try to find Lloyd.” She sits but cranes her neck to see the Ritter, no longer tugging on her ear. Keeping her within my sight, I call the emergency number I have for the Hawkins and the daughter in Waukegan, Illinois, picks up. I explain who and where I am and that I have Mrs. Hawkins next to me.

“Oh, OH! Thank god!” comes the relieved voice. “You have my mother!” she sniffles. “We’ve been so worried!” she gasps. “Her memory care residence called me yesterday when she didn’t come to breakfast and we’ve been sick with worry ever since!” She excuses herself to get a tissue.

“M’am, I’m looking for Mr. Hawkins here in the airport but…” I get no further when she interrupts.

“No, no,” she says. “My father, Lloyd, died about two months ago. When he got sick, he told me he’d have to cancel the trip. I guess he didn’t. My mother forgets everything. I don’t know how she remembered or how she got on the plane?” I tell her about Lilly’s rendition of Stormy Weather in the Duty Free Shop and the security guards.

“Oh dear,” she gasped. “Was she arrested?” No, I tell her, they left her in my care. “My mom used the name Lilly on stage,” she explains. “She was a headliner in jazz clubs in Chicago and cabarets in New Orleans. She loved that life, that world. She breaks into song all the time in her care home.”

I look over at Mildred. Now in her late 70s, she still had the voice that commanded an audience, if not a grasp of reality. “Can I speak to her please?” I hand the phone to Mildred who asks at least four times who “this” is. The first three times Mildred tells her she doesn’t have a daughter but something breaks through on the fourth try and I see her smile.

After some minutes of Mildred just listening she hands the phone back to me. The daughter tells me she will be on the next flight to Frankfurt. I explain how to find us in the city.

"I'm going to get some of that," Mildred says as she points at the Ritter chocolate. On our way she stops and stares at the crate of Canadian Club. In one quick step, she's on it again, hesitates, then raises her face into the brilliant track lights. She lifts her arms and breaks into another torch song. This time it's Lady Sings the Blues. In one transformative instant, Mildred is Lilly again. She's back in her own reality, where she's young and happy, safe and warm.

To hell with security, I think, as a new crowd begins to form. Let her have this moment. Her voice soars across the hall, her face tilts into the rapture of the song. She's in a New Orleans cabaret, belting out the lyrics, far, far away from here.

Cardinal Sins

Mike Nemeth

Oscillating blue and red lights shone through the dirty sheer curtains on the front window, interrupting our boisterous conversation and laughter.

"Oh, crap!" Eli said. Ready to flee, he sprang to his feet and pulled his wife up from the battered green leather couch.

"Police!" a man yelled while pounding on the front door.

"Too late to run," Eddie said.

He moved to the door and looked through the small window. A tall, hollow-cheeked man in a checkered sport coat did the pounding. Beside him, a thick Black man with closely cropped hair wore shades although the sun had already set. The black cop wasn't tall, but he was thick and muscular, like a football running back. He wrote on a clipboard while the white cop glared at Eddie through the cracked window.

"Open up!" the white cop said.

The duplex had no driveway so two squad cars, a small paddy wagon and one unmarked land yacht huddled on the weed-infested lawn. The paddy wagon driver leaned against his rig nonchalantly, arms folded.

"The door is broken," Eddie shouted. "Go around back and I'll let you in."

The cops exchanged looks. They hadn't brought a battering ram.

"I'll let you in the back," Eddie assured them.

The white cop stationed two uniformed cops on the tiny front porch. He and the black cop hustled around the side of the duplex followed by two more uniforms.

Eddie turned away from the door and surveyed the room. Eli and his wife, Tiffany, had resumed their seats on the couch. Ricky and his underaged girlfriend—Eddie thought her name was Amber or Crystal, something pole dancers used on stage—stood next to Eddie's roommate, Cole, near the kitchen. The teenager was holding a sixteen-ounce glass of crushed ice and Jack Daniels. Eddie grabbed the glass and gave it to Cole who scratched his head.

"Stay calm and we'll be okay," Eddie said to the room. He walked through the cramped kitchen to the back door that opened onto a porch. On thc adjoining porch, behind the other half of the duplex, the little weasel-y guy, Damon, threw something into the backyard, gave Eddie a scared look, and disappeared inside like a chipmunk ducking into its tunnel to evade a predator.

The uniforms appeared from the side of the duplex, vaulted onto the porch and shoved Eddie inside. They herded Eddie all the way into the living room and took up guard positions blocking the kitchen and the doorway to the bedrooms. The gaunt white cop ambled in and announced that he had a search warrant. He instructed everyone to remain in the living room while the two uniforms searched the bedrooms and the single bathroom. The black plainclothes cop then took the kitchen apart one drawer and one cupboard at a time while the white cop stood watch in the living room.

Tiffany stifled a chuckle as the toilet in the other half of the duplex flushed repeatedly. Cole gulped the teenaged girl's drink and shuffled from one foot to the other.

The black plain clothes cop tired of dumping food containers and dishes into the sink. The two uniforms reentered the living room and shook their heads. The white cop said, "Search them and put them in the kitchen."

One at a time, Eli, Tiffany, Cole, Ricky, the teenaged girl, and Eddie passed through hand searches by the uniforms on their way to the kitchen. When everyone was jammed into the tiny space, the uniforms searched the living room. There wasn't much to search, a TV cabinet and the shabby green couch, but a few minutes later, one of the uniforms shouted, "Found it," and ran into the kitchen to show the white plainclothes cop what he had found, like a bird dog bringing its master a dead pheasant. In his hand he cradled a ball of silver tinfoil.

"It was between the cushions of the couch," the uniform said.

Carefully, the plainclothes cop unraveled the tinfoil to reveal stems and seeds, a few crumpled leaves. "Well, well." He stuck his nose close to the greenish brown vegetation and sniffed. "Mary Jane, for sure," he said.

The plainclothes cop looked from one cowering person to another. "Whose is it?"

Eyes downcast, no one responded. Cole started to point a finger, then thought better of it.

"Okay," the white plainclothes cop said, "who lives here?"

"Cole and I do," Eddie said, pointing to the big man squeezed between the table and the refrigerator.

"Okay, everyone else out of here."

Ricky, the teenager, Eli, and Tiffany scurried out the back door. The black cop took IDs from Eddie and Cole and recorded their names on a form on his clipboard.

"You're under arrest for possession of a controlled substance, to wit: marijuana," the white cop said.

"Why? It's not ours," Cole said.

"It's on your premises, so it's yours. Ipso facto," the white cop said with a gleam in his eye.

"That's ridiculous," Eddie said. "We weren't sitting on the couch."

"It's the law," the white cop said.

The black cop shrugged.

“Let’s go.” The white cop took Eddie’s arm and led him out the back door. The black cop escorted Cole, the bigger man who could cause a problem. The cops ushered the two young men into the back of the paddy wagon and the driver slammed the door shut. Through the back windows, Eddie saw Eli, Tiffany, and their weasel-y roommate standing on the porch of the other half of the duplex where they lived.

As the paddy wagon made its way to the Savannah city jail the driver said, “Y’all stationed at the base?”

“Yes, sir,” Cole said. “Just back from Nam.”

“You, too?” The driver meant Eddie.

“Yeah, me too.”

“Well, the country is proud of you for doing your duty but y’all shoulda kept your noses clean. You’da been back home in no time. Now ya gonna be a guest of Uncle Sam in a different way.” He shook his head like it was a sad shame.

***

At this hour, the jail was nearly empty. The cells were arranged back-to-back in one long row with a solid steel spine down the center and steel side walls. Bars on the fronts and ceilings of the cells reminded Eddie of the cages for the big cats at the circus. A jailer locked them into the second cell from the front on the inside row. To the left in the 8’x8’ space were anchored bunk beds, to the right a shiny steel commode. One prisoner at a time could stand in the leftover space. Eddie stood.

Cole sat on the lower bed, his elbows on his knees, face in his hands. “It wasn’t even ours.”

“It won’t stand up in court.” Tired of standing, Eddie climbed onto the top bed and stared through the bars at fluorescent lights.

“I was never scared over there,” Cole said.

“Nam?”

"My daddy was in the big war and he survived because he knew he would die. Once you accept it, he said, you're never scared. I got there, I said to myself, 'Cole, you're gonna die in this shithole.' After that I was never scared."

At 6'2" and 230 pounds, Cole was the obvious choice in his platoon to carry and operate the heavy, awkward M60 machine gun. The machine gun was the most powerful infantry tool and therefore the machine gunner was the primary target of the enemy.

"I was scared all the time," Eddie admitted.

"You were in the lap of luxury at Long Binh. I'll bet you went to movies, sat by the swimming pool, played tennis, and spent your nights at the NCO club. That place was like a Caribbean resort."

"That's the point: I had hoped I could survive a year and that's what causes the fear that you could be hit by a random rocket or mortar shell. Sappers blew up the ammo dump while I was there, and I had to go to the wire with my M79 grenade launcher. Scariest night of my young life."

"Well, I'm back in my own country and now I'm scared."

***

Around midnight the prisoners began flowing into the jail at an accelerated pace and the noise level escalated. Arrested for public intoxication, assault, petty theft, possession or sale of narcotics, these criminals were the detritus of Savannah's late-night streets. The murderers and other violent offenders were sent to the more secure County lockup.

Because of the noise, and because all the new prisoners were marched past their cell at the entrance end of the row, it was impossible to sleep. In the early morning hours, the drunks and the regulars bailed themselves out and the noise abated. Eddie and Cole were finally able to get some rest.

***

Midafternoon, a guard came to get them. “You have a visitor.”

In a small room they sat on one side of a table with a divider down the middle. On the other side sat a disheveled man with patchy baldness wearing a brown and yellow sport jacket that might once have been a horse blanket. The sweat stained collar of his aqua shirt was open revealing sprouts of black neck hair over a carelessly knotted brown tie.

“Who are you?” Eddie said.

“I’m your court-appointed counsel. Name is Roger Hoover. Don’t have much time ‘cause Saturday mornings are busy.”

“When do we get out?” Cole said.

“Your bad luck to be arrested on Friday night. Sunday through Thursday are the good days because court’s in session Monday through Friday.” He grinned, showing his crooked teeth.

“Lots of people got out this morning,” Eddie said.

Hoover leaned back and blew air. “Sure, traffic court and municipal court. You guys are headed for Superior Court. You’ll be arraigned Monday morning and the judge will set bail. I know some good bail bondsmen.”

“We shouldn’t be here,” Cole said. “Wasn’t our pot.”

Hoover shrugged. “According to the law, what’s on your property is yours.”

“So what’s our defense?” Eddie said.

“Oh, first offense, GI’s who served their country. Your pot weighed in at less than a gram so no intent to distribute. Should be the minimum sentence of two years in the State pen.” He shrugged again.

“Sheeit. I can’t do that,” Cole said. “I just did a year in the jungle.”

Hoover checked his Timex watch. "Gotta run, see some more clients. I'll meet you in court on Monday morning. If you can't make bail, you'll be transferred to the county jail. You don't want to go there, believe me."

Back in their cell, Cole said, "You know it was Eli's. No one else was on that couch."

"Ricky and what's-her-name were making out on it earlier."

"They're alkies, not heads."

"Damon had been on the couch before he left to use his own toilet because you wouldn't let him use ours."

"He's a scuzzy little sucker. Don't want his dirty butt on my clean toilet seat." Cole scratched his head. "He's a dealer. Think he'll admit it?"

Eddie didn't have to answer the question. "My theory is that they had intended to raid Eli and Damon but everyone was in our side of the duplex so they changed their minds. The black cop was writing on his clipboard when I went to the door, like he was changing 245A to 245B in the address."

"Just our luck."

***

By Sunday afternoon they had run out of fresh things to say to one another, so they welcomed the news that they had another visitor. Eddie expected it to be one of his neighbors. Instead he was surprised to find Captain Butch Waters, their company commander, waiting for them. Cole was happy to see him. Eddie was Cole's roomie but Butch was Cole's best friend. They both came from NASCAR country—Appalachia—Cole the western North Carolina mountains, Butch the part of Virginia that butts up against Tennessee. Their interest in cars wasn't shared by Eddie. Cole's pride and joy was a Camaro SS with the big engine and a four speed on the floor. He bought it through the PX with his tax-free wages and combat pay while serving in Vietnam. Butch owned a

Chevelle SS with the same kit. The two of them would park their cars on the lawn and then talk about them or polish them for hours.

Butch listened to their drug bust story and said, “I can cover for you tomorrow. I’ll sign a three-day pass. But if you’re not in formation Tuesday morning, Top will report you AWOL.” By ‘Top’ he meant the company’s First Sergeant, a no-nonsense Army lifer.

“I have two Purple Hearts and you’re gonna let that lifer report me AWOL?” Cole said. “I thought we was friends, Butch.”

Butch held up two hands—stay calm. “I’ll do what I can.”

“If we don’t get out tomorrow, it won’t matter what the Army does to us,” Eddie said. “We’ll be in the county jail until our trial and then in prison for two years.”

***

The Chatham County courthouse doesn’t resemble the stately cupola-topped, red-brick-and white-columns, halls of justice emblematic of the Old South. A steel and glass, six story rectangle on Montgomery Street, the courthouse could be the headquarters of any Fortune 500 company.

In three-days-old civilian clothes, no handcuffs, Cole and Eddie stood before an elderly white judge who did not feign interest in their case.

Hoover, their court-appointed attorney had urged them to plead guilty and throw themselves on the mercy of the court. There was always the chance, he had said, that the judge would give them a suspended sentence. Eddie suspected the lawyer simply didn’t want his calendar clogged with another trial.

When asked for a plea, Eddie said, “Not guilty, your honor,” in a clear, composed and steady voice. Cole followed suit. In a droll, disinterested voice, the judge swiftly scheduled their trial for a date two months away, set bail at $1000 apiece, and remanded the prisoners to the Chatham County jail. The entire proceeding lasted less than five minutes.

The officer who had delivered them to court escorted them into a bustling corridor. "They've made bail. I'll take 'em back to City and process them out."

"How'd that happen?" Hoover said.

"Don't know," the officer said. "Someone posted bond for them."

"Woohoo! We made bail," Cole said. He punched Eddie on the shoulder and let out a Rebel yell that attracted stares from lawyers, defendants and cops.

Eddie expected to find that Butch Waters had opened his checkbook and posted bail. He was wrong again. A bail bondsman had been hired by Eli Watson for ten percent of the bail amount, the remainder due if Cole and Eddie skipped bail.

"Told ya it was Eli's grass," Cole said. Why else would he spend his money to bail us out?"

Their neighbors were waiting for them in the parking lot. Damon apologized for not coming to visit them in the city jail. "Had to sell a few bags to raise the bail money," he said with a laugh. Ironic, Eddie thought, to be bailed out of jail with drug money. Cole swiveled around to give Eddie an I-told-you-so look.

First thing Eddie wanted was a shower; second thing he wanted was a nap in his own bed. But Cole insisted they stop for Whoppers and a chocolate shake. We all have our priorities, Eddie thought.

At work the boys found they wore invisible scarlet letters, marking them as criminals under indictment. Their elation at being released from jail was quickly replaced by gnawing anxiety and suffocating depression. Time passed inexorably. Calls to Hoover, the attorney, went unanswered.

On a weekend in the middle of May, Cole drove his Camaro to North Carolina to mothball it at his mom's house and Eddie had the apartment to himself. Sunday afternoon, Lorraine, the secretary who worked with him on base, appeared on Eddie's doorstep. Eddie had ignored her attempts to get his attention and yet, here she was. He guessed she had come from church, wearing a dress and comfortable heels and conservative makeup. He directed her around the house and met her on the back porch.

"Hope you don't mind that I came unannounced."

"I don't mind, just surprised." He cleared his throat and swept his arm toward the door like a matador. "Please."

She ambled past leaving him in a cloud of subtle perfume.

"Excuse the mess. GI's live here," he said.

She chuckled, looked around the cluttered kitchen and passed through to the living room. She moved a stack of magazines aside so she could sit on the couch. Eddie sat beside her on the couch. Then he bounced back up and said, "Can I get you something to drink?"

"You probably only have liquor," she said, as though she was excited to be in this den of iniquity.

"Believe it or not, we have iced tea."

"Sure, that'd be fine."

Eddie poured the tea, handed her the drink, hesitated, then sat beside her again. He didn't know what to say.

"You probably wonder why I came to see you."

He nodded.

"When I first heard of your arrest I was very disappointed, Eddie. I always thought you were a nice boy and it broke my heart to find that maybe you weren't … a nice boy."

What was he supposed to say to that? "Our mistake was mixing with some bad friends."

"Hm hmm. That Eli is a bad boy. From California so what do you expect? Was his pot, wasn't it?"

"That's what Cole thinks. Anyway, we're running out of time and our lawyer has been no help at all."

"That's why I came," she said, as she dug a folded newspaper clipping out of her purse and handed the clipping to Eddie.

The story recounted a drug trial in which a Fort Stewart GI had been acquitted in Chatham County Superior Court. His attorneys, a father and daughter team named Morris and Rebecca Sokolov, were quoted as saying that the Savannah police had conducted an illegal search and seizure violating the Fourth Amendment to the U.S. Constitution.

Eddie handed the clipping to Lorraine and shrugged. “Lucky guys.”

“They do it all the time, Eddie. They know how to manipulate the law. They know how to get soldiers out of trouble.”

“You think we should hire these people?”

“That’s what I would do.”

He folded the clipping and slid it into his shirt pocket. “I’ll see what Cole says when he gets back from North Carolina.”

Her smile spread slowly, like a milkshake spilled on a flat surface. “You shouldn’t be alone with something like this hanging over your head. I’ll keep you company.”

Peaches and cream complexion—a Southern specialty—sleepy blue eyes, bee-stung lips. He wondered why he hadn’t noticed before now. “Why don’t I treat you to lunch, pay you back for this.” He tapped his shirt pocket.

“Thank you, but I had something at church.” She kicked off her shoes and folded one leg under her on the couch. “When will Cole be back?”

That’s what Eddie wanted to know.

***

Cole rode a Continental Trailways bus from North Carolina to Savannah and arrived after dark Sunday night. When he found Lorraine cuddled up to Eddie on the couch, he said, “Excuse me, ma’am, don’t mean to interrupt,” and scuttled off to his bedroom.

“I’d better be going,” Lorraine said.

Eddie walked her through the kitchen onto the back porch. Before she took the steps to the yard, Lorraine whirled and kissed Eddie on the lips.

He hadn't tried to seduce her. Eddie guessed right, had proven himself "a nice boy."

When she was gone, Eddie showed Cole the newspaper clipping. On Monday, he made an appointment to meet the lawyers.

***

"I got no money to waste on a lawyer, Eddie. I give my money to Mama, you know that. She needs me to come home and take care of her."

They were in an elevator, rising to the seventh-floor offices of Sokolov & Sokolov, Attorneys at Law.

"You're not going home with Hoover representing us."

Wood paneling, plush carpet to suppress noise, hushed conversations, no sense of urgency or desperation in the sedate office, but moisture on Eddie's palms as he and Cole waited on a black leather couch. After fifteen minutes, the receptionist led Eddie and Cole down a hallway to a small conference room. Yet another five minutes passed before a woman, tall, blonde, mid-thirties, and shapely, in a light blue dress and heels entered the room. She looked like she was ready for a lunch date with her boyfriend. She took a good look at the boys as she dropped a file on the table and introduced herself as Rebecca Sokolov.

She paged through their arrest record, noted that the arresting officers were Thomas Dunlap and Herman Jones. Raised her eyebrows at that. "Tell me what happened in your own words."

"We got screwed," Cole said. "It wasn't our weed."

Eddie patted Cole on the arm and explained that as NCO's they had permission to live off base and that made their apartment the center of social activity for their circle of friends. He went through the events of the night of April 23, their interactions with Hoover, their arraignment and their bail release. Rebecca didn't interject, just took notes.

Eddie floated the idea that the search was intended for the other half of the duplex, but the cops changed their minds when they saw that everyone was on their side. Rebecca pulled a sheet of paper from the file and scanned it. "The affidavit from the C.I. that was used to obtain the search warrant didn't specify a side of the duplex."

"C.I.?" Eddie said.

"Confidential Informant."

"Who's the rat?" Cole said.

"Someone in trouble with the cops who traded this information for a plea bargain."

"What? Someone we know?"

"Shouldn't the affidavit have been specific? Two different groups of people live in that duplex," Eddie said.

Rebecca canted her head. "The judge probably didn't know it was a duplex, was told it was a residence. Maybe the C.I. knew that people usually gathered on your side of the duplex."

Cole snapped his fingers. "That's why the cop said, 'Found it!'"

Rebecca's right eyebrow shot up, waiting for Cole to explain.

"He knew he was supposed to find a ball of tinfoil because it had been planted."

Rebecca's left eyebrow joined the right. She took a note.

"Wait here. I want my father to meet you." Rebecca left the room. Eddie thought they had passed a test.

***

Morris Sokolov had a narrow, craggy face, and white hair swept away from his forehead and over his collar in back. He moved in ragged jerks, as though suffering from arthritis. He sat and folded his hands on the table. Rebecca took a seat and listened as Morris walked the boys through their histories—high school, college for Eddie, service records, Cole's Purple Hearts, all about their families. He didn't ask a single question about the drug raid.

Satisfied, Morris said, "We'll take your case. Our fee will be $500.00."

"What are our chances?" Eddie said.

"We'll get you off," Morris said.

"Because that affidavit, from the C.I., is pretty shaky, right?"

"Leave the legal work to us," Rebecca said.

The boys leaned back in their chairs, traded questioning looks.

"I ain't got it," Cole said.

"I'll get it," Eddie said.

***

"Shysters. They're gonna take your money and we're still going to prison."

"You got a better idea?"

"Run to Canada."

"I think you have to file as a conscientious objector *before* you kill a hundred enemy soldiers."

"Not like that. Just hide out in the Yukon."

Eddie scoffed at him. "Take your mama along, pitch a tent for her? Teach her to cook over a campfire? Wrestle bears—"

"Shut up."

***

"You've always been a disappointment to me. Now you're a disappointment to your mother."

Eddie's mother, on the bedroom extension, sobbed.

"This is fixable. I just need $500 for the lawyer fees."

"You don't have $500 to your name?"

“On E-5 pay? I have rent and a car payment, utilities. And I eat, for God’s sake.”

“I told you to go to Officer Candidate School, but you wouldn’t do it.”

“Sure, I could have been the first guy killed in an ambush. Military funeral, twenty-one-gun salute. Gold Star parents.”

“Always the drama. You’ve made your bed, now sleep in it.”

Eddie’s mom stopped the debate. “Give him the money, Harold, or I’ll make your life a living hell.”

Unnecessary threat, Eddie thought. His parents already made one another’s lives hell.

Heavy breathing as Eddie’s father tried to decide how to save face. “It’s a loan, Eddie, not a gift. You understand? You’re an adult and it’s not my job to support you. When you get out, I’m the first person you pay back.”

I should sell some grass to raise the money, Eddie thought. “Okay.” Eddie gave his father instructions for sending the money to Sokolov & Sokolov.

***

Two weeks passed without a word from Sokolov & Sokolov. “I told you they stole your money,” Cole said. Finally, Rebecca Sokolov called Eddie at work. “We need to talk. Leave Cole at home.”

Eddie asked Lorraine to cover for him, snuck out of the warehouse in the middle of the afternoon and went to the attorney’s office in his fatigues. In the same small conference as on their first visit, Rebecca Sokolov sat across from Eddie wearing a serious look.

“We’ve discovered that you aren’t on the lease for 245B 66th Street.”

“Cole was already in the apartment when I got back from Nam. I replaced some guy who got out of the Army.”

“We can separate your cases, have you tried individually. We’ll make the argument that you aren’t responsible for what the lease holder has on his premises. You’re no different from the other people who were visiting on the night of the search, people they let go and didn’t charge.”

Maybe Mom’s prayers have been answered, Eddie thought. “What are the chances?”

“You’ll get off.”

“What about Cole’s chances?”

“Less than 50/50.”

“So, our chances together are less than 50/50? Your father said you’d get us off.”

“I’ll come to that but give me an answer first.”

He flushed with shame for considering the cowardly betrayal of his roommate. He dropped his head into his hands, massaged his temples, rubbed his eyes. He felt like a man trapped on a carnival ride, strangling the seat restraint bar with sweaty hands, doomed to finish the ride, hoping without reason that the ride would end safely.

After a long moment he said, “I can’t do that to Cole. It wasn’t his pot.”

Rebecca smiled, seemingly pleased with his answer. “We know how to get your case dismissed but we have to hire an investigator to gather the physical evidence to take to court.”

Eddie wasn’t sure what sort of response was expected of him. He shrugged. “That’s great.”

“The investigator’s fee is $500. We’ll need the money before we can go back to court with a motion to dismiss.”

“Oh, God.” Cole was right, the Sokolov’s were shysters milking a naïve GI of his money. “You have no idea what I go through to get your money.”

“This is your ticket to freedom,” Rebecca said. “Don’t miss the train.”

***

“You’re an idiot. You’ve been scammed.” Cole took a beer from the refrigerator and flopped onto the couch, next to Lorraine.

“Can you help with the money?”

“Nope, don’t have any.”

“You gonna just lie around until we get sent to prison?” Eddie said to Cole.

“Nope,” Cole said, and he winked.

“What have you and Butch been up to?”

“What the cops should have done from the beginning.”

***

His mother answered the phone, but his father tore the receiver away from her. “Calling to tell us where we can visit our son in prison?”

“We have a way out. The lawyers need another $500 for an investigator to collect physical evidence.”

His father guffawed. “Told you how this would go. The lawyers are bleeding you to death.”

“This is our last chance. Will you give me the money or not?”

“Give him the money, Harold,” his mother said.

“I knew this would happen. I’ll give you money but there’s a quid pro quo. Know what that is, Eddie?”

“I know what a quid pro quo is.” He thought of *The Merchant of Venice.*

“When you get out of prison—because that’s where you’re going—you won’t be able to get a job from anyone except me. So, here’s the deal: you come back home, live in my house in your old bedroom, and work for me. That way I can garnish your wages and get my money back.”

“Doing what?”

“You’d have been useful if you had studied accounting or marketing, but you had to go for English Literature, so I’ll put you on the machines. Can’t have an ex-con on the counter, meeting customers. How’s that sound?”

It sounded worse than prison. Eddie’s father owned a dry-cleaning store. Machine work was sweaty, mind numbing, soul crushing work. Maybe that’s what he deserved.

“It will be so nice to have you in the house,” his mother said.

***

Three more days passed with no word from the Sokolov’s. He and Lorraine were on the couch when they felt as much as heard a massive thump! The wall behind the couch, the wall between Eddie’s apartment and the other half of the duplex, shivered and the pictures on the wall bounced on their hooks. Lorraine slid away from the wall, to the edge of the couch, and grasped Eddie’s bicep. “What was that?’

Before he could answer, something heavy hit the wall again and one of his pictures fell behind the couch, its glass shattering when it struck the floor. Eddie jumped to his feet. He heard muffled shouts followed by a scream, a male scream.

“Call 9-1-1,” he said to Lorraine.

He hustled through the kitchen and across the connecting porch to the other back door. Another scream came from the apartment—not a scream of fear, a scream of pain. He bumped into chairs in the tiny kitchen as he rushed inside. On the floor of the living room, Cole sat on Damon’s chest, a bayonet—the one he took off a dead North Vietnamese soldier—held high over his head by his cocked right arm. The bayonet dripped blood.

“Get off him, Cole. You cut his femoral artery.”

“Hunh?” Cole said, as though in a daze. He looked over his shoulder toward Eddie and then he saw it: blood pulsing from Damon's left thigh in spurts, like a miniature geyser. "I didn't mean to stick him." Cole rolled off Damon.

"Well, he's going to die."

Damon moaned. Eddie whipped off his leather belt and knelt beside the little man. He slid one end of the belt under Damon's leg then through the buckle. He stood and yanked the belt loop tight and secured it. Damon screamed again. The blood stopped spurting from Damon's leg, but his face had lost its color.

"They set us up, Eddie. Butch found the list of soldiers had been arrested, guys who might roll over on other GI's, and we surveilled them. It was a gung-ho buck sergeant out at Fort Stewart. And guess who he sells his dope to? This piece of crap."

Eddie took a giant leap of logic. "The soldier in the article Lorraine gave me. He was represented by the Sokolov's."

"Yeah, they got him off by informing on us and this weasel planted the pot. I was gonna make him admit it."

Lorraine screamed as she entered the living room, her hands to her mouth. Two whoop, whoops of a siren and flashing red and blue lights alerted them to the arrival of help.

"You called the cops?" Cole said to Lorraine.

"I called an ambulance," she said.

But the cops were the first ones through the door, followed by two MP's. Cole dropped the bayonet and the cops cuffed him. The MP's looked on, fingers hooked in their weapons belts, stolid, as though they had been invited to witness an oil change under a shade tree. The cops told Eddie and Lorraine to move to the kitchen—"Don't touch anything"—and wait for them to return. They dragged Cole out of the apartment as the ambulance finally arrived.

Lorraine obeyed the cops, but Eddie waited with Damon.

"Good job on the tourniquet," one of the paramedics said to Eddie. "Saved his life." They stretchered Damon and wheeled him out the front door. He was groggy from loss of blood.

Eddie walked alongside. "Was Cole right, Damon?"

Damon nodded. "I was going to put the pot in the toilet tank, but Cole chased me out of your apartment. It wasn't my pot they found."

"I know," Eddie said.

The cops questioned Eddie and Lorraine before carting Cole off to jail. They hadn't witnessed the stabbing, but Eddie had seen Cole sitting on Damon's chest, threatening the man with the bloody bayonet. That would be enough to destroy Cole's life.

***

Eddie heard nothing from his lawyers for a week and assumed he would go to trial alone, that his last chance was to be considered a bystander on the night of the drug raid. Then his phone rang two days before his court date and Rebecca's paralegal said, "You can come down and pick up your court order."

"Court order?"

"Sure. The case against you and Cole has been dismissed."

Lightheaded, floating like a helium balloon, he drove downtown and took the elevator to the seventh floor. At the receptionist's desk he asked for Rebecca.

"She's busy." The attractive receptionist handed him a single sheet of paper. "That's it, your court order."

Through the glass wall behind the receptionist's desk, he saw her, talking to the black cop, Herman Jones, the one who had written on the clipboard on his front porch. Eddie walked into the waiting area and read the court order. The case had been dismissed because the search warrant was "invalid on its face." No city or state had been listed. "245B 66th Street could be in New York City," Rebecca had argued, and the judge had agreed.

***

Lorraine was ecstatic, jumping up and down, laughing and crying and hugging her hero. "Let's celebrate!"

"I'm not in the mood," Eddie said. His initial elation had drained away like water down a bath drain when he thought about Cole in a County jail cell.

"You think the Sokolov's bribed a crooked cop to mess up the search warrant, don't you?"

"I do. That's where our $500 investigator fee went."

"I think it's a scheme they work all the time to save GI's from a stupid law. You can't feel bad about getting off this way."

He gave her a thin smile. Cole had survived a year in the jungle evading VC and the NVA, so Eddie assumed the brave warrior could withstand the pressure of a pending trial for two measly months. He was wrong. Selfishly, Eddie had concealed the truth, hoping disclosure would never become his only option and the poor kid had self-destructed. That's what he felt bad about.

Mrs. Arbuthnot Makes a Donation

Patricia Feinberg Stoner

'I suppose it's that time,' sighed Clarissa Mainwaring, spying through the kitchen window as the ungainly figure of the vicar trundled up her front path.

'Goodness me,' she went on, 'the Reverend Cedric is putting on weight. I suppose while Mrs Rev has been away looking after her poorly sister, the Rev has been eating far too many ready meals. We should have invited him over more often.'

Professor Mainwaring rattled his *Guardian* and pretended to look fierce.

'Nonsense! Once a week was *quite* enough, dear. One can only take so much "For what we are about to receive." And now, as you say, it's that time, and here he comes trotting up the drive to rope us into the annual Bring and Buy. And as usual, I suppose, you'll do most of the work and he'll take all of the credit.'

His wife sighed again. 'You know it's for a good cause, dear. And this year, especially, with those poor refugees.'

'Refugees be blowed,' said the Professor rather uncharitably. And then, recollecting himself, he added hastily, 'Oh, I know, it's different this year. It's not as if it were hordes of perfectly fit and able young men trying to get into this country to blow us all up.'

Clarissa rolled her eyes but said nothing. She and her husband had had many a lively debate about refugees, but on the subject of the Ukrainians they were as one. The little village of Gorehampton had recently welcomed Alina, who had fled to the UK with her eight-year-old daughter Katya and baby Marko, tearfully leaving her husband Artem behind to fight the Russian invaders. Mrs Plumpton, the greengrocer's widow, had taken them in a few weeks earlier.

'It's company for me, now my lovely Eddie has gone,' she explained. 'And those poor mites are so bewildered and lost, it breaks my heart.'

The Reverend Cedric had a soft and charitable heart. Every year he pondered and prayed hard over the question of whom the church Bring and Buy sale should benefit. His own leaning was towards the homeless, mainly out of a vague feeling of guilt: he and his wife had a bijou hideaway in the Lake District, where they took their annual holiday. It was slightly unfair, he thought, that he and his wife should have two homes when others had none. He would have welcomed a Ukrainian family, but the small and inconvenient vicarage was already crammed to bursting with himself, his wife, his four children and two dogs.

There had been a parish meeting, but the outcome was never in doubt. This year the proceeds from the sale would be divided in two: half to go towards whatever help was needed in Ukraine, and half to support their own village refugee family.

In her cottage on the north side of the Green, Mrs Arbuthnot was contemplating her winter wardrobe. What could she bear to part with, she wondered, before packing it away for the summer. It wouldn't be long before the cheeky Jason—self-styled ambassador from village to Arbuthnot—would beat a path to her door. He'd be after a donation, she knew, and this year she would be ready for him.

Sure enough, when he arrived, two carrier bags of slightly pilled sweaters, an elderly red handbag, a pair of scuffed brogues and some worn but serviceable unmentionables from Damart sat on the kitchen table ready for collection.

'And I shall want those carrier bags back, mind, Jason,' said Mrs Arbuthnot sternly. They're 'bags for life' from Marks and Spencer and they cost me £1.20 each.'

'Right you are, Mrs A,' said Jason cheerfully. 'I don't suppose you were thinking of putting the kettle on?'

Mrs Arbuthnot shot him a look, and he grinned.

'Didn't think so,' he said, and picking up the carrier bags he left, unrefreshed.

Mrs Arbuthnot didn't usually do village events. They were too full of pushy mothers and overexcited children with sticky fingers. But even her flinty heart had been touched by the horror in Ukraine, which she followed assiduously every evening on the 6 o'clock news, and she had even, when no-one was looking, had a friendly word for Alina and her family. Perhaps this year she should make an exception?

It had been a glorious summer so far, but the day of the Bring and Buy sale dawned cloudy and a little chilly. Mrs Arbuthnot, who had only recently packed her depleted winter wardrobe away in mothballs and lavender, decided to retrieve The Coat. This was a special favourite of hers, a soft navy-blue wool with white trimmings; it had been an absolute bargain at £7.50 in the Kitty Rescue shop in Hortlesham last year.

She set off for the parish hall resplendent in The Coat, but by the time she reached the Green she was beginning to regret her choice. Although still overcast, the weather had warmed up considerably, and it was a red-faced and breathless Mrs Arbuthnot who arrived at the Bring and Buy sale.

Every table was a-bustle with eager volunteers: the kiddies' clothing, the tombola, the cake stall, the white elephant, the preloved apparel, the bargain books. The entire population of Gorehampton, and many from beyond, it seemed, swarmed through the hall on the lookout for bargains and tittle tattle.

Spotting an empty table at the very back of the room, Mrs Arbuthnot gratefully deposited her coat and dived into the fray. Scraps of conversation floated past her.

'Did you see, dear, Mrs Jenkins has finally got rid of that most unsuitable hat…'

'I swear that was the vase I gave her last Christmas…'

'Who on earth would donate, ahem, *undies*?'

'Oh dear, I see Mrs Jenings has brought those dreadful rock cakes…'

Once round the hall, Mrs Arbuthnot decided, and then a cup of tea with a scone which, she knew, would be vastly inferior to her own baking. But it was for charity after all. But just as she was bearing down on an unclaimed table near the refreshments counter, Mrs Arbuthnot stopped dead in her tracks.

There was Alina, Katya in tow, baby Marko asleep in a sling on her back. And over her arm was The Coat. Enid Arbuthnot's very own coat!

Mrs Arbuthnot glanced over to the empty table where she had left it, but the table was empty no more. Martha, the vicar's wife, newly arrived back from her sisterly visit with an armful of donated clothing, had commandeered the table and the coat with it.

'Alina, that's my coat!' cried the bereft Mrs Arbuthnot. Before Alina could reply, Martha appeared on the scene, also in search of tea.

'Oh, was that yours?' she said. 'Such a very generous donation, thank you.'

'Yes, and such a bargain,' Alina chipped in. 'I only pay £5.'

For once in her life, Mrs Arbuthnot was speechless.

The Pilgrim

Colette Lynch

Halcyon days of endless summer playing with my brother in our immense garden, watched over by our parents, sipping tea on the veranda. That is how I would like to recall my childhood, but in reality, Peter and I were the youngest of seven, so no-one minded us. Apart from our souls, our bodies were left to our own devices. We were in awe of our older brothers, who seemed to exist as a collective in their own right, completely separate from ourselves. It was not just the significant age difference. They were Numeraries and lived in the Opus Dei house, united with God and elevated from the rest of mankind. We did not use their sibling names. They were referred to as 'them.'

"I want to be like 'them' when I grow up," said Peter. " To be holy and good, to be special."

"Well, you'll have to be cleverer than you are," I said cruelly. "They're all very smart. Daddy always says that if they had not been called, they would have gone to university and could have been anything they wanted."

"Do you think they could add?"

"Of course, anybody can do that. They were probably able to do big sums in their head without using their fingers."

What did I know? I was six, but I wanted to hurt my brother.

Our primary school was Catholic, not Opus Dei, but we had daily Mass, learnt our catechism, developed an unhealthy fear of

God who could divine everything and saw your deeds before you committed them. In order to make it through a day as a good child, you had to be ever-vigilant. My brother had high standards in relation to goodness and was terrified that he would be damned and sent to hell for all eternity.

"It has come to my notice," said Brother Francis, "that some boys are forgetting God's watchful eye. You may think you have gotten away with not learning your catechism because the teacher did not ask you a question, but God sees. To remind you of the punishment that awaits those who transgress, I want you to experience what the fires of hell will be like."

He lit a candle.

"Thomas O'Riordan come up here."

Thomas, a redheaded, bespectacled child, sloped to the front.

"Put your finger into the flame."

"What Father?"

"You heard me, "he said, seizing Thomas's minute digit and pushing it into the fire. His screams, no doubt, gave his tormentor great satisfaction.

"Ow, Father that hurts. Me finger's burning."

"Exactly. That's how much the flames of hell will hurt."

Thomas ran to his seat, blowing on his scorched finger. This litany was repeated every day, so it was inevitable that at some stage it would be your turn.

"Peter Diaz, I noticed you yawning during our class on obedience so perhaps this will wake you up. Come up here."

The candle flickered. To my deep shame, my brother started to cry. We were only seven, but even at that tender age, it was an accepted truth that tears were for girls. Brother Francis, delighted by this reaction, swooped down upon Peter like a black crow in his priestly robes. He dragged him up to the front and held three of his fingers into the flame until my brother was almost collapsing. I was determined that when it came to my turn, he could put my entire hand into the flame until it burnt to a cinder before I would show any emotion.

Brother Francis was not the only sadist. Brother Xavier who taught Maths and Irish, had a store of imaginative punitive measures. Once again, my brother was an embarrassment.

"What is 16 plus 24 Peter Diaz? How long are we going to have to stand here for? No Joseph, you cannot help him."

My brother stood, face burning at the blackboard. I wanted to throttle him.

"Go and put your head in that bin because there's nothing but rubbish in it."

As instructed, he knelt down and stuck his head into the receptacle.

"Now cough."

The class was trying badly to suppress their laughter. Peter did as he was told. The dust flew up, choking him. His asthma made this an even more dramatic event.

"Brother he can't breathe," I said.

"Do you think I'm a fool? Sure I know he can't breathe. He can't add either."

On reflection, perhaps it was these trials which my sweet-natured brother had to undergo that primed him for his future life as an aesthete and a Numerary in the Opus Dei house. With a year between us, we could not have been more different. I was constantly having to defend him, as he felt it was ungodly to exert violence.

"If you say that again about my brother, I'll punch you. "

"Come on then. Yous darkies are a pack of wimps."

In fact, my brother was pale, but that distinction didn't matter to Seamus, the basher Mullan. We were pulled apart by an irate brother, and our punishment was to stand holding hands, our noses pressed to the window of the classroom for the rest of the day. My daily defence of my sibling continued. I was always coming home with some part of me bloodied and bruised.

"Why can't you be more like your brother?" said my mother. "Look at the state of your uniform. I'll never get it clean. You have to try harder to control your temper. Look at Jesus. Even when he was being tortured and humiliated, he accepted his pain without violence. Fists are never the answer."

Christ didn't have a brother, was all I could think.

It did not stop for us when we got home from school. Other kids could go out and play or read their comics, but we had to endure Mother's interrogation.

"What did you learn today children?"

Peter would begin.

"Well, we went to Mass and then did our lessons. I came first in the Catechism test. I knew all about God and His angels and saints."

"I helped Peter with his sums because the teacher was cross with him."

We were vying for attention.

"That was good Joseph. Why didn't you tell me the complete truth about your day Peter, instead of just the parts that made you look good? You know God detests liars. Instead of going outside, you will sit here and write out 100 times. 'I will not displease God. I will always be truthful."

I felt bad, but not bad enough.

Preparing to take our first confession was a torturous time for my brother. He spent days examining his conscience and listing his sins. I always said the same thing.

"Father, bless me for I have sinned. I disobeyed my parents."

I had finished my penance at the altar while my brother was still there 15 minutes later, his small head bowed in supplication. I have no idea what sins he had manufactured.

From the ages of five to 11, my father was an imposing but congenial figure. Our mother was the focal point of our lives.

"You are the youngest boys, and you have a lot to live up to," she said. "Following in the footsteps of your brothers requires diligence. You must never waver. Do not listen to what your friends say at school. Some of them are not brought up in the way of good Catholics. We, as servants of Opus Dei, are sanctified. Without our faith, and the support of our church, we would not be what we are today, and you would not have this comfortable home. Goodness has its own rewards."

My mother had no joy, but I longed for it. She was 16 when she met my father, a worldly man 14 years her senior. He was already established as a successful businessman in Dublin and his Spanish roots made him revered in Opus Dei circles. She was serving buns in a local café when he encountered her and, in her version, saved her life. Her job was to give birth to children and rear them. Their achievements were her successes. Failure was not an option. She followed The Virgin Mary, and our house was full of shrines. The one girl that she produced died at birth. She would have been the last child, and no doubt my mother's age had to do with her demise, but she blamed herself for her body's treachery. Her depression drove her to locked rooms, and it was Peter's job to cajole her out.

"Mammy, please come out. I need to tell you what happened at school today."

He would sit timidly, knocking at the door until, in desperation, she would exit.

"Is this all you can do with your time? The devil finds work for idle hands. Come with me and I'll keep you occupied."

Pulling him by the ear, she deposited him at the table. Overseen by the glowering figure of my mother, he would spend the rest of the evening learning passages from the founder of Opus Dei, Saint Josemaria Escriva's books. It did not appear to me that goodness had its own rewards.

As we reached puberty, our father took over.

"Joseph wake up! I'm covered in sticky stuff. Something's leaking," said Peter in hushed tones.

I looked at his pyjamas and saw the creamy residue. I put my fingers in it, sniffed and tasted its saltiness.

"I don't know what it is, but don't let Mammy see."

He hid his pyjamas and that night the cloth was stiff.

"Maybe you spilt something, and you don't remember. The same thing occurred the following night, so we decided that the only solution was to tell our mother. He begged me to take the blame. For a handful of marbles, I complied. Our mother threw the offending articles on the floor.

"You are an obscenity," she said to me. "If you were closer to God, this would not happen. Take these away from me and go to your father. You are no longer my child."

I told Peter that when we went to see our father, he would have to own up to whatever his misdemeanour was. This marked a transition period for us.

"Now Peter," said Daddy. "This also concerns you Joseph. You are becoming young men and that is the stage when the Devil starts his battle with your bodies."

We were terrified.

"You must not let your physical urges control you. You are the master of your bodies, not the other way around. Peter, you have had an involuntary ejaculation."

I automatically took my brother's hand. This must mean he was dying.

"Is Peter going to be with God?" I said.

My father laughed.

"No nothing as dramatic as that. It's perfectly normal. The stuff that is on your pyjamas is semen."

"Like being in the Navy," said Peter, totally confused.

"It sounds like that, but it is semen, not sea men."

He spelt it out.

"Semen contains sperm and that is what is needed to make babies when you're married. Your penis is becoming active, and you have to control its function."

I wanted to take my penis out there and then and have a good look at it, but wisely decided to leave the inspection until later. What had previously been a feature of peeing was developing a personality of its own.

"How can I stop it Daddy?" said Peter, crying.

"There's no need to get upset son. All men have to deal with this. Take a cold shower before you go to bed, and another one in the morning. Pray more than usual and God will help you. If it happens again, wash your pyjamas yourself. Do not subject your mother to this indignity. Under no circumstances be tempted to touch your penis. "

"How will we pee Daddy?" I said.

"Sit down."

Peter looked relieved at being given a solution. I heard from boys who had sisters that this is what girls did, and I resolved to disobey my father. At 10, my fall from grace had begun.

Peter had no friends at primary school, but I had plenty. They would invite me over to play in their houses at the weekends, but I was never able to go. Our Saturdays and Sundays were dedicated to God. I kept this information to myself. It was bad enough to have Peter as my brother. I realised what was normal and saw that we were far from it.

"I love the Opus Dei club. I feel at home here, not like school. These kids are really nice," said Peter as he sat hunched over a jigsaw of Noah.

I was bored and wanted to be somewhere, anywhere else. The really bad thing about these thoughts is that I didn't feel bad about them.

In secondary school, Peter found his place. We attended an Opus Dei led school. He was lauded for being a nerd and found fellow companions. He unlocked calculus and joined the chess club with Daddy's permission. I discovered the bike shed, smoking and masturbation. The road to hell was paved with enticing acts of rebellion. At 13, I was well on my way to being irretrievably lost.

"Were you pulling on your oul bod last night?" said Micky to Pat.

Along with the others, I laughed conspiratorially, although I had no idea what he was talking about and was relieved he hadn't addressed me. I sucked on my share of the cigarette to give me something to do. I had mastered this art and no longer spluttered when I inhaled.

"Yeah. I was thinkin' of your Ma."

Later in the garden shed which had become my personal Hades, I yanked at my penis but could not understand the purpose as it produced no effect, not even when I thought of Pat's mother, although I noticed it getting firmer. I was doing something wrong, but it's not like I could ask my father. I had a good friend, Cathal, who had a similar background to myself and was also delving into the dark side. We'd bonded in primary school when, during the Opus Dei club, we both agreed that we would rather play football.

"Look, I found a book in the central library," said Cathal. "It had pictures and everything. I tried it out, and it worked. I mean, it's bad, like, no doubt, probably the worst thing I've done. I made the mistake of confessing it to the priest, and he went mad. I thought he was goin' to tell my father. He told me I would go to hell if I did it again, and he came out of the box and thumped me around the head. I was mortified. Everybody was looking. Of course, I faced the Inquisition from my parents who had been sittin' in the church."

"What did you tell them?"

"I said that I had stolen a pencil. They had a major prayer praying session, and I was sent to bed without supper. They're watching me all the time now."

"Anyway, how did you do it?"

"You move your hand up and down your bod, and as you feel it get bigger, stuff comes out and you feel great. It takes a wee bit of practice but keep at it. It's definitely worth it. Just don't tell the priest."

He was right. Nothing that felt this good could be sinful, or that was my reasoning. I developed a duplicitous nature. Peter was praying enough for both of us, so I managed to slip under the radar. I joined a lot of after-school classes, always checking with my father first and didn't attend any of them. Instead, I hung out with the boys whose parents had sent them to the school for their education but had instructed them not to be indoctrinated by the priests. The corner shop was the hub of iniquity, and that's where I met Roisin. She was the first girl I had kissed, having practiced on my hand once I learnt that French kissing had nothing to do with the language. She was also the first girl I fell in love with. In fact, I never felt that way again, not even with my wife. Her hair fell in dark curls down her back and her eyes were impossibly large. They looked violet in certain lights and her lashes were so long I loved the feel of them on my cheek. Her skin was soft and cream coloured. In the summer, she was brown. When I first met her, she had her school skirt pulled up and her knee socks turned down. I could not take my eyes off her legs. It seemed unimaginable that someone as beautiful as her would be remotely interested in me, but she was. Together, we discovered sex and, after that, there was no turning back. I would have given my life for her. We planned to marry and spent hours discussing our future.

"You want to do what?" said my father. My mother had collapsed in a heap.

"You are 16 years of age with your whole life ahead of you. This is my fault. I gave you too much trust and freedom. I expected you to be like your brother but you have strayed.

"He's damned," said my mother, as Peter cradled her.

"You have been tempted and like Adam, have succumbed. I need to speak to you in private," said my father.

Throughout this tirade, I had remained resolute. Roisin and I would not be separated. I sat opposite my father and the profound look of sorrow on his face shamed me.

"Joseph, I need you to be honest. This is a difficult question for me to ask and I fear your response but do not lie. Have you been fully intimate with this girl?"

"If you mean, did I have sex then the answer is yes, I love her."

My father stood, and without a backward glance, left the room. I was to be exiled and to discover the impotency of 16-year-old dreams.

I had gone to bed after my revelation, only to discover that Peter had removed himself from my presence and had taken up residence in the guest's quarters. When I awoke the next morning, I couldn't open the door.

"Open the door. You can't do this to me," I said, kicking at the wood.

"You can make as much noise as you like," said my father, "but you are going nowhere until your soul is shriven, no matter how long that takes."

They kept me in there for three weeks, during which time I was given water and bread. That's the only time I saw a human being. The door would be opened, and I was held back by two men whom I did not recognise, as my brother left a pail and plate. It sounded like there was an entire congregation praying outside the door, begging the Lord to save my soul. My soul did indeed ache but not from the loss of God but from the absence of Roisin.

On the evening of the third week, my father opened the door. I was weak but made a dash to escape. My exit was blocked by a barricade of people. I turned in despair to my father.

"Daddy, I know I have failed you, and I'm sorry, I really am. I never meant to hurt you, but I love her, and nothing will change that."

"You are my son, and it is my duty to save you. You have been blinded by carnal lust and I must help you to see. You are not the first young man to stray from The Path. You are lost but you will be found."

He told me to face the wall, whereupon I was blindfolded. I struggled, but to no avail. My hands were tied behind my back and my feet shackled. I did not know where I was being taken. I was shouting, so they gagged my mouth. After some time in a car, I could hear the sea, the horns of ships and I was being pushed up a gang plank. The ship started to move. I was choking on my own vomit when the gag was removed. At first I couldn't see anything. My father lit the candle. It was just him and me. I didn't move. There was no point. I had no control over what was happening. My destiny was no longer mine.

I didn't know where I was going or how long I would be on the boat. I was scrubbing the deck, climbing the mast and emptying slops. I learned how not to kill myself on my ascent and descent of the pole, and how to avoid the contents of the bucket slapping me in the face. For the two-day journey, I never saw my father. He joined me as I stood waiting for the ship to dock.

"This is Bilbao," he said.

"We're in Spain?"

He nodded.

"Where are we going?"

He did not respond, nor did he look at me.

"Are you not going to tell me? Don't I have a right to know?"

"Here's how this is going to work. You will know your destination when we reach it. It will be a long journey during which I want you to observe and contemplate. Think about what brought you here. Your thoughts are your own and I do not wish to hear them. We will proceed in silence. These are the last words I will speak to you."

He turned, and I ran after him. Bilbao reminded me of Dublin, although I thought my city was prettier. There was a sense of violence, and it was difficult to manouevre through the crowds and not lose sight of my father, who never once checked that I was there. We took a bus to Madrid. The heat was relentless, and the sweat poured into my eyes, making it difficult to focus. I was hungry, but food was evidently not on the agenda. My father gave me a bottle of water, which I gratefully received. On perusal, the city was beautiful, and I wanted to pause and look at the plazas, but stopping was not an option. The next bus we took was to Granada. My father bought us more water, ham and bread from a kiosk, and we ate in silence on the bus. It was getting dark, and I fell asleep. I was taken aback by the snow on the mountains when I woke. Granada was very different from the other cities. The air seemed cleaner. We had breakfast in the cafe and I hoped that this would be the last stop. Father paid and left with me in his wake. Another bus journey lay ahead. We had been travelling for 20 hours. The landscape began to change. We were going further away from civilisation. My anxiety rose. After about an hour, the bus stopped in a place called Pitres, which seemed to have nothing but a church and a cemetery. In the centre of the square was a wagon with two horses. An old man stood beside the horses. He raised his hand in greeting to my father. They embraced. The old man turned to me and in Spanish said.

"Hello Joseph. I am your grandfather."

I expected my father to stay, but instead he turned to me, putting his hand on my shoulder.

"I do not know when I will see you again son, but this is your opportunity to find yourself and the love of God that you have lost. You will know when you're ready to come home. I leave you a boy in expectation of the man you will become."

He kissed me and left. For the first time in nine years, I felt like a child again. I turned my head so that my grandfather would not see my tears. We got on the wagon and began our trek through the mountains. I had become used to silence, which was just as well as my grandfather was not given to small talk. We arrived in

Altabeitar, which was to be my home for the next three years. I wondered how I would spend my time in this place as there was nothing but some stone cottages, a church and the ubiquitous cemetery. It was similar to the last village, except this one was even smaller. There were no cafes, restaurants, cinemas, or arcades. Nothing but a local bar.

"We will water the horses and then continue," said Grandfather.

My Spanish was fluent, but the Andalusian dialect was unfamiliar to me, so it took some time before I fully understood what was being said, but it was clear that our travelling was not over.

On the other side of the mountain lay Grandfather's farm. It was huge and full of men engaged in activities which were foreign to me. The first few weeks I slept with the sheep and then was gradually accepted into the workers' hut. Miguel was my instructor. He was a few years older than me, and we became friends.

"OK Jose," he said. "Let's get something to eat. Do you smoke?"

I nodded and accepted. Over food, he described the farm.

"Senor Diaz has the biggest property in the region. He has sheep so we produce milk, cheese and of course meat. We also make our own sherry which is sold throughout Spain. We grow corn, tomatoes, chilies and cucumbers. Of course, we also make our own olive oil. You might think that this place is dead, but you'd be wrong. There are fiestas every week here, lots of music, drinking, dancing and pretty girls but be careful."

He didn't need to warn me about that. I had learnt my lesson.

"We pray in the mornings before we start our day and then in the evenings when we return. Take a wander around and tomorrow you will start with harvesting the olives."

I sat on a tree stump, stunned by my surroundings and the rapid changes to my life. I realised that I had not thought about Roisin for three days. For the first six months, my grandfather did not speak to me other than to issue instructions. Then one evening, Miguel told me he wanted to see me at the house.

"Sit Jose," said my grandfather. The table was laid with breads, cheeses, olives, hams and a variety of other dishes which I did not recognise, so presumed must be local. There was also wine and water. I expected not to be served alcohol, so I poured myself a glass of water.

"Here, you're old enough. Have some wine"

As we ate, he talked.

"I have been watching you, Jose. You are a good worker and a quick learner, two essential attributes for a farmer. Your milking skills need some work, but they tell me that you can manage to get something out of the teats in less than an hour. However, practice makes experts of us all. Someday it will come together, the sheep will no longer dance away and in an hour, you will have milked three sheep and the buckets will be full. It's the same with life. When you least expect it, things make sense. How are you finding things?"

"It was very strange at first, but I really enjoy working with the animals. I love the feel of the earth and before I came here, I had never seen fields turn silver in the dawn. I am going to shear my first sheep tomorrow, so I am looking forward to that. Miguel and me are going into the village later for the start of the fiesta."

"That's good. Work is important, but also so is enjoyment. That's enough talk for now. We will chat again."

I wanted to ask how long I would be staying, but it did not seem an appropriate question. Time was ceasing to have any meaning. One evening, many months later, as I was minding the sheep, my grandfather joined me.

"You know, Jose," he said, "I'm a very old man and I have lived several lives. I have killed men and cured them."

I was shocked. "You killed some-one?"

"Yes many. I fought in the Civil War on the side of the Nationalists. I was a young man about your age. I left my family and joined up. I wanted to do something meaningful, and I loved my country. One afternoon I was sitting in the Square eating bread, my hands stained with the blood of my fellow countrymen when I was joined by a fellow dressed like a tramp. His trousers were held up with string. I shared my food, and we fell into conversation. That moment changed my life. Do you know who he was?"

"No. Who?"

"Josemaria Escriva."

I was dumbfounded. Up to this point, there was a part of me that doubted his existence and yet my grandfather had met him.

"Why wasn't he dressed like a priest?"

"He was in hiding from the Republicans. If they had found him, they would have killed him because he was a priest. He told me that when he was 16, he saw footprints in the snow outside his bedroom window. They had been made by a Carmelite monk and Josemaria wondered how he could show his love for God, what could he offer? What can you offer Jose?"

"I don't know. I've never thought about it."

"Perhaps you should. You know, he told me a story that really affected me and completely altered my thinking. A man wanted to erect a cross at the crossroads of his village where his brother had been murdered. Josémaria advised him against it as the sign of the cross was one of love, not revenge or hatred. He said that saintliness was not the preserve of the canonised. Those of us who discover the call to holiness in our everyday life and work, are sanctified. Saint Bakers, Saint Tailors, Saint Farmers. Isn't that a great thought Jose? What could be better?"

"I suppose it is," I said.

"I know why your father sent you here. You sinned but you are not condemned. You can learn from your experience and resolve to become a complete person, loving, compassionate, intelligent and moral. Prayers are a way of giving thanks and communicating with Jesus but they are only one way. When you watch the silver dawn you are talking to Him. Nothing is more satisfying than sharing God's love with others and helping them to find it. Think about these things."

His words had meaning for me. My grandfather was not a saint. He had done bad things, but yet if what Josémaria was saying was right, despite his actions, he was a saint in his everyday life. He had found his path and everything he now did was done in God's name. He had showed me the beauty of God's creation and had given me time to appreciate its worth. I asked Miguel how he saw his future.

"I have not told you this. Only your grandfather knows my true story. None of it was my fault but I still feel ashamed of it. Well, ashamed of the things it drove me to do. My mother got pregnant when she was 19. She wasn't married and her parents would not support her. Instead, they put her in a prison for nursing mothers in Madrid. I found this out when my father was dying. Before that I had no idea that I had been adopted. A lot of the young girls in that place were told that their babies had died but that wasn't true. They were sold to a couple who couldn't have kids of their own and that's what happened to me. I was reared in Granada as an only child. My upbringing was strict and my father was a cruel man. He never showed me any affection. We had money and a big house with servants. I had never known poverty. Before he died when I was 14, he told me that I was not his son and he regretted ever having adopted me. He said that my birth mother was a prostitute and that he had bought me from a priest because his wife and he could not have children. He wanted to give me as a gift to her. He believed she would tire of me, but she loved me. As soon as he drew his last breath, I took some money from his drawer and ran away. I think now that this was a cruel thing to do to my adopted mother, but I was angry. I had been lied to you know? I travelled on the trains and when my money ran out, I stole from shops, robbed people, begged on the streets and one time sold my body to an old man. That was the worst time of my life. I suppose you think I am trash now."

"No Miguel. I am thinking how lucky I have been and how I wasted my privileges."

"So, I was begging in the square in Granada when your grandfather started to talk to me. I didn't really trust him but he persuaded me to go with him. I figured I had nothing to lose. The worst had already happened to me. I was the same age as you when you arrived here. He did not ask me about my story but just accepted me as I was. He gave me work, my self-respect and time. At first, I didn't pray but as time passed, I found the words comforting. I realised that I had been blaming God for what had happened to me when the fault was not God's but the men who had lied and used me. You ask me what I want now for my future. It's simple. I want to share the love and peace that I have found. I want a wife, lots of children and work the land, always helping others as I have been helped. Become a Saint Farmer."

He laughed.

"Bet you're sorry you asked me now."

"Come on," I said. "You need a beer."

His tale deeply affected me, and I began to see my life in relief. I had no idea what real suffering was and had been too arrogant. I should have been grateful for the ease of my existence and thanked God for my good fortune, but it was never too late.

Many months later I returned to my favourite spot to watch the sun set. I heard the cicadas rubbing their legs, the sheep bleating, my own breath. I was filled with a peace I had never before experienced. It was not just the silence. This tranquillity came from within, and I recognised the feeling as one I had had before. Then it was physical and bound in time, but this sensation was spiritual and universal. It was love for nature, love for mankind, love for myself, love for God.

"You're back," said my father rising from his chair and hugging me.

His tone was congenial, as if I just returned from an errand in the city rather than three years in Spain.

“Let me look at you. Yes Joseph. I can see you have been transformed. You shine with conviction. I am so proud of you”

“Papa,” I said, “I know I cannot be a Numerary because of my transgression but I want to dedicate my life to helping others find the inner peace I now possess.”

I will never forget the look of pleasure and relief on his face as he grasped my hand.

“Let us begin,” he said.

Bamboo Sonnet

Karen Miller

You kissed me ‘neath the bamboo’s thicket tall
Our passion sang amidst its rustling leaves
We pressed our ears against its woody wall
To hear the bamboo quaff within its sheaves.

The bamboo grows a foot or two each day
Its thirsty constitution we revere
And revel in its cool and lofty sway
The shade from our own bamboo belvedere.

The bamboo lives and grows one hundred years
If only you’d be mine that long times ten
Through all our love and laughter and our tears
I’d love you one more thousand years again.

No matter what the bamboo’s apogee
It shan’t outgrow the love I have for thee.

Nursery Road

Linda C. Rehkopf

Sweat trickles through the pink-clay dust on my forehead and neck and cheeks, where my bobbed blonde hair doesn't cover my skin. I am eight years old, and the summer is hot. We wade the creek, watch the horses in the pasture, get bored with that, and start another epic dirt-clod fight with the boys next door.

A drainage gully of clay, where grass sprigs surrender by midsummer and even wildflowers and weeds refuse to make a stand, separates our houses in a neighborhood claimed partly from pasture and partly from an orchard. The backyards are still wild with brambles and thickets, but an intrepid crew staked four-foot chain link fence around each perfect square of yard. In the front yards, pecan trees drop nuts, and apple trees spit big round fruit from gnarled branches in the fall.

Culvert pipes wend under the new streets, and one of us fits in this perfect hiding place, two if we crouch. Down the slight incline at the end of the gully between our house and the boys next door is the chain link fence, the "safe" zone during dirt-clod fights. Anyone sitting atop the fence is off-limits. The goal is to make it from the culvert to the fence unscathed.

Even eight-and ten-year olds have standards for battle. A throw to the head means an automatic expulsion from the game. A direct hit to the torso is a kill, but arms and legs are mere amputations. Rocks and dirt-clods embedded with rocks are forbidden.

I could not throw a dirt-clod in a straight line to save my life. My skills are speed and agility while I run zigzagged along the gully, or sometimes crawl through the dirt to draw the enemy from their positions behind the apple trees, so my teammates can lob clay with precision.

The chain link provides a toehold for my sneakers, and I am about to swing a leg over the top rail and yell "Safe!" when a dirt-gravel clod hits me upside the head. I grab my temple and burst into tears and make that scream that children make that brings parents out of the house.

I try to get untangled from the chain link fence, but at the same time protect myself from the righteous number of dirt-clods coming at me. Most of them dissolve to pink dust on my bare skin, streaked now with sweat and tears.

The boys next door laugh; I am almost stunned at this flagrant flaunt of the rules, but more at the openly cruel tactics. I watch one of the boys wind up and cock his arm, ready to throw another rock, when my father reaches him. "What the hell?" I heard from my dad as he grabs this enemy boy, takes the rock, sends him home, and lifts me from the fence, almost in one action. He sets me on the ground, wipes the grit from my hairline. "Quit messing with those boys."

We lived in a square brick house in a neighborhood surrounded by small farms and barbed-wire-protected plots for horses and goats. The property had been the site of a Civil War battle. Occasionally, musket balls and rusted buttons and sharp-edged arrowheads vomit up from the yard. The clay didn't lend itself to growing grass or flowers, but my mother tried. The street we lived on, Nursery Road, seemed to hold on to the land's former life and resisted change.

My brother and sister and I were the new kids, transplants from the North, in 1962. It rained so often that first summer, our mom threatened every day to move back to Jersey. We took advantage of rain delays to have indoor play dates, and we made new friends with kids up and down the street. During the dry mornings, our friends and playmates taught us wonderful things: how to ford a creek, how to catch crawdads. We learned where to dig for sassafras roots after bulldozers had scraped another lot for a new home, how to soak the roots in water and chew the bitterness out of them. Honeysuckle—white and yellow and some pale pink—wound around fence posts and trailed along the top rails. Our friends taught us to pluck the delicate flower at the base, pull the black-tipped stamen from the center of the bloom, and suck the sweet nectar.

To our left on Nursery Road was a family with two girls. We played Barbies and school, and wrote and performed backyard plays with sheets on the clothesline as our curtain. We made popsicles in the ice cube trays using grape or cherry Kool-Aid. My play clothes were always stained, either from popsicle drips or from the red clay we played in.

Their father worked at a plant that made cardboard and wood boxes, which he occasionally brought home. We stacked packing crates into multi-level forts in the backyard, cut squares for windows and rectangles for doors. We drew curtains and flowers on the outsides of the boxes.

To the right of our house in another square brick house, the family had two boys. A huge Confederate Stars and Bars flag hung on the boys' bedroom wall, an X that we could see from our yard. Those boys carried matches in their jeans pockets and knew how to light our summer-night sparklers.

During all our childhood adventures, our dog Dixie always came along.

Dixie was a gentle, quiet bundle of German shepherd mix that my father brought to us on a hot June day, two weeks after the birth of my youngest sister. Back then, dogs roamed freely despite the fences. Dixie was no different; she was our sidekick and our friend and our protector, but she was a traveling dog.

My dad could stand in the front yard and whistle, and she'd come home immediately. His whistle for the dog was distinct—with two fingers to his lips, he'd blast low and long with the final note higher, trailing off. (Dad's "kids get home right this minute" whistle was more shrill and punctuated with breaths, a loud Morse code carried on summer breezes.)

Each of us had assigned feed-the-dog days. I usually talked my sister or brother into letting me have their dog chores, and I would fill Dixie's bowl with Gravy Train, pour warm water over it, and watch the clear liquid turn a milky-brown. I sat on the kitchen floor, leaned against the cabinet door, and hand fed her.

"One for you," I said, and held out a kibble in my pudgy hand. Dixie gingerly took the food between her front teeth and chewed. "And one for me," and I chewed a piece (just to be sure the water wasn't too hot). She knew I wouldn't hold any morsel back, and that she would get most of the meal.

I was eight years old this magical summer of Dixie's puppyhood and our younger sister's infancy, when Dixie followed my other siblings and me up and down Nursery Road, over the fences, between the trees, across the creek.

Playtime always included Dixie, and we were required to watch out for the dog. In the spring and summer, during epic red clay dirt-clod fights, nobody got to hurt Dixie, and it was our responsibility to make sure this never happened.

The day the evil boy broke the battle rule, my father reached him before Dixie could. Though I was not sure, at that moment, which would have been the worse option for that kid, I still remember feeling protected and vindicated. I am sure I taunted those boys with a smile when Dad set me on the ground.

Our father was the cool dad. A telephone systems engineer, he brought home spools of grey-insulated wire that we stripped to separate all the colored strands. We twisted the red and blue and yellow and green wires together and made jewelry. Moms up and down Nursery Road sported their children's creations, the rings and the bracelets and the necklaces.

Most of my father's colleagues were transplants. All of them were friends of our parents, and their children became our friends. We vacationed together and took picnics together. We did not all go to school together, though. The Black kids had their school, sometimes many miles away, and their school buses were as shabby as the buildings that housed the elementary and high schools. We had our neighborhood school, a new building a few blocks away from our house.

By 1968, with four kids and a dog in a three-bedroom house, Nursery Road began to suffocate us all, and a larger house a few miles away was built. In between deciding tile and wallpaper and linoleum options, and when the Nursery Road house was for sale, my mother helped Dixie whelp her only litter. The brown, fluffy puppies had black-tipped ears that flopped at odd angles, just like Dixie's.

I don't remember too much about the puppies, but I do remember one of the families that came for a dog for their kids. The father was one of my dad's colleagues. While we kids played with the pups in the front yard, the adults talked inside, out of the sweltering heat. Shortly, they made their pick and took home one of the fat pups, the brown one that was the same color as the family. I thought it was neat that the puppy's fur matched their skin.

I don't think my sister and brother and I ever noticed that our playmates that day were Black. I don't think we ever talked about the differences between us. We were happy one of our puppies went to a good home.

It wasn't long—maybe an hour—before the phone calls began.

My mother paled suddenly; all the color drained out of her face and she sank into a chair. She sent us down the street to a neighbor's, and we had an unexpected sleepover. Mom made excuses: she had a doctor's appointment, you have to go now, Mrs.

Hall or Mrs. Lanier will babysit you, she said. Mrs. Lanier had introduced me to the guitar, and I watched her pick and strum chords while she sang the songs of the mid-1960s: protest songs and peace songs and folk songs. I wanted to be like her and sing like her and play the guitar like her.

But on the day of the telephone calls, Mrs. Lanier did not pick up her instrument. Instead, she held us and closed the drapes and probably made cookies in the kitchen in the rear of her house.

To this day, Mom will not speak about those menacing telephone calls, will not repeat the words said to her on the telephone lines that my father helped develop.

I remember clearly this next part, because the bedroom window opened up to the street. A fire late one night out on the lawn threw yellow flames that threatened the mailbox and a sad patch of blue morning glories.

Someone poured gasoline in the grass and threw a match. The next morning we could see the shape in the scorched yard—an outline of a cross. Dixie, gone missing, crawled home later with her backend full of buckshot.

It didn't make sense to me then, in our small, segregated neighborhood clawed out of farmland with pecan trees and apple trees and azaleas lining Nursery Road. But I knew, on some level, that an invasive species had crossed a line.

I remember thinking, was this because of the dog?

My father was furious. It wasn't because of the dog, he said. I didn't believe him. We had a dog that had puppies. We gave a puppy away. My mother sent us to the neighbor's house. A cross was burned in our yard. That was the chain of events, and I was 10 years old by then, so my logic was linear.

I had not been immune to racist comments during my childhood. I just never understood them. When my grandmother, herself a first-generation Polish-American, would tell us as we played on her Perth Amboy, New Jersey porch, "Watch out for the Puerto Ricans," I wasn't sure what to watch out for. Was a Puerto

Rican a poisonous plant in the side yard, a wide sidewalk crack, a stinging insect to avoid? As far as I was concerned, while I skipped or jumped rope or bounced a tiny red rubber ball during a game of jacks, I had never encountered a Puerto Rican. "Oh, that was close," I used to tell myself if the ball bounced too close to the outside basement steps.

Two blocks away from my grandmother's house, but 43 years prior to my birth, the Ku Klux Klan had tried to meet secretly in my hometown. Word got out, and 6,000 rioters rooted 150 Klansmen out of the Odd Fellows Hall in Perth Amboy. The 1923 newspaper accounts called it the largest anti-Klan riot, ever. The town's police and firemen, who tried to keep the Klansmen safe from a public lynching, were overrun; their weapons were confiscated, and the fire hoses that had been trained on the crowd were slashed. The rioters were Jewish, Catholic, Black, White, Puerto Ricans. They linked arms and formed human chains to prevent the Klan members—some still in their white robes—from escape. Some of the Klansmen were beaten. Nobody died.

* * *

Many years passed before I connected dots: our house was for sale, and a Black family visited. Had the fire been set, and the phoned threats made, because our dog had puppies, because a Black family had visited? Had the fear of integration of Nursery Road finally sparked that violence? Even more years passed before we talked about it in our family.

But on the day I saw my father clenching his fists in the yard, then digging out the burnt grass, I knew he was standing up for Dixie and her puppies and our right to give them away to whomever we wanted. And if my father was going to stand up for the dog, then I would, too. This is the moment that I understood my responsibility, when I learned about empathy, when I saw the power of hate and the only possible response to that hate.

This day was different from the day my grandmother warned me about Puerto Ricans.

I was afraid. I was afraid for Dixie. I was afraid of the boys next door. I wet my bed and had nightmares, which embarrassed me, so I stopped spending the night with other little girls. I quit going to the kids-only fort in the woods. I rode my bicycle with my small hands firmly gripped on the handlebars. I didn't share my spooled wire so often, and I began to check out more books from the traveling Bookmobile.

Those vile boys, who never obeyed the rules of the dirt-clod fights, and their pocked-faced father, had dribbled gas in a sacred pattern on our patch of grass. They threw the match. They probably watched.

"They were always setting things on fire," my brother said decades later. Indeed, one of the boys had set hisownself on fire. We had listened to his screams from across the gulley through the open windows while his parents changed his burn dressings.

Not long after the day the puppy left us, when Dixie wandered home with a backend full of gunshot, my father stood defiant and angry in the street that afternoon and called out at the neighbors, the mean kids who stood on their front porch, and their pock-faced father behind them holding a gun in the crook of his arm. "Any coward can shoot into the hide of a defenseless dog," my father had screamed. "If you're a man, you put that gun down and meet me here in the street."

They crept back into their house, and maybe looked out to see Dad still in the street, pacing, running his hands through his thick dark hair.

We escaped the street and the hatred in the summer of 1968, loaded the car and a moving van, and took Dixie.

There is no police report, no official record, of the violence on Nursery Road in Smyrna, Georgia, in the spring of 1968. "Who would I have called?" my dad asked me. "Who do you think they were?"

What did I know then about the power of a dog to inspire, to frighten, to help, to comfort? What did I know then about the ability of a dog to illuminate the pettiness or the vengefulness of our neighbors? What did I know about hate, until that night when the Ku Klux Klan boys and their father threw a lighted match onto a gasoline-soaked, social sore spot?

How did my own hometown's history fail to travel with us on the long drive down the coast, from New Jersey, through Baltimore and Raleigh, through small towns and larger cities, to Atlanta? Did the story jump generations?

Perhaps the details of 1923 live on in the coded DNA of the dogs we have loved over those decades. Perhaps the memory DNA of an ancestor in Perth Amboy lives on in me.

I did know one thing, one small thing, after that night: I would always stand for the dog.

When people ask me, now, why my dogs play such an important role in my life, I think about Dixie, about the cross burnt into wilted grass, about the phone threats, about my family's response. I think about Perth Amboy, New Jersey, and the warnings all through my childhood to watch out for the Puerto Ricans. I think about 1923, 6,000 men of all races and heritages, locked arms, saying to the Klan holed up in Odd Fellows Hall, "Not in my town."

Burtrell's Pieces

Jeff Clemmons

Burtrell's desire for Lorraine started long before he loved her. In fact, twenty years into their marriage and nineteen years after his desire had tempered, love remained little more than an inkling of an idea simmering on the back burner of his unconsciousness. It wasn't until their firstborn died in childbirth - Lorraine rising every morning against her grief to bottle feed their newly orphaned grandbaby - that Burtrell, whose heart had broken into a hundred tiny pieces, began to love his wife.

Worse Than Murder

Mike Coleman

"If you're thinking about copping a plea, forget it," says Winton Lanier III, dapper in his blue-and-white-striped seersucker suit. "Don't you trust your old buddy Win to get you out of this mess?"

"You haven't lost a case in thirty years," I say, accepting one of the beers he has brought me. It's not very cold, but that's okay. "It's just that …"

Win studies me while he takes off his jacket. Then he stands in front of the window air conditioner, arms held high, a sweat ring at each armpit. There has never been a need to stand on ceremony with each other. Except for one thing. "It's just that what? If you've got something to say, Boyd, say it. I can't get you an acquittal without knowing all the facts."

I lean against the bedroom door frame of the apartment Linda kept in town, or more rightly the one I paid for so she could "have her space." It's where I've spent every day since I killed her a week ago, here in this apartment. It happened last Friday, about this time of day, when the thick August twilight turns everything purple, and darkness is still a couple drinks away.

"Saw Clive Smith at the club today. Said to give you his regards." Win pulls the ruffled stool out from under the French provincial vanity Linda bought when she furnished the place, folds his lanky frame onto it.

Any other time I'd laugh, tell him how silly it looks for a man six-foot-two to perch on the frilly little thing. "What did Clive have to allow?" I ask.

"He's pulling for you, Boyd. People know what Linda was. And they know you deserved better, the man whose column has made it worth getting out of bed in the morning for the last twenty years."

"It's men who like my column. Women think I'm a sexist pig. You know the Virginia Slims crowd. 'You've come a long way, baby' and all that. You've seen their letters to the editor. Even Winton Lanier III can't get me an all-male jury. Those ladies'll take one look at my flabby, fifty-year-old ass and cheer Linda on for what she was doing." My stomach burns at the thought of her and Ed in bed together.

Win plants his long shiny shoes a good yard apart on the dark green carpet, swivels back and forth on the stool while the beer can crackles between his palms. I know he's worried about me spending my days and nights in this place since he bailed me out of jail on Tuesday, worried I'll slip another cog before going to trial for the murder of my estranged wife. It's why he's checked on me every day since my release, brought me beer and groceries and the paper when I've asked for it. We've known each other since grade school.

"I'm liking the idea of building your case around the struggle with the knife," he says. "Lucky you told the police you're not sure how the thing got in your hand, Boyd. Linda had it first, didn't she? Took you by surprise? Killing in self-defense is justified if you're under attack with a deadly weapon." He scratches his chin. "Only thing, in Alabama you've got to show you couldn't get away."

"Well, then," I say vaguely.

Unfazed, Win continues. "What did lover boy Ed tell the police? That he was zipped up and out of here before he saw anybody do anything with any knife. There's our window for reasonable doubt right there, Boyd. Linda was ten years younger than you. Strong. Willful. Look at the way she scratched you up."

I don't have to glance at the scabbed-over tracks of her fingernails on my rusty-haired forearms to know they're still there. "I'm bigger than she was," I counter. "And I stabbed her four times."

"Being made a fool will do that to a man. You, the jealous husband, tired of your wife's shenanigans, come to try to reason with her one last time. Only to find her in flagrante delicto with the other man. You went a little crazy."

"Correction, counselor. I was never so clear-headed in my life."

"Tell me what's on your mind, Boyd!"

At last, he's out of patience. I take another sip of beer and begin.

***

Afterward, Win's voice is all incredulity. "Now let me get this straight," he says. "On a Monday night four months ago, Ed tries to pick *you* up at the Cloverleaf Grill?"

"He did pick me up."

"You—and the fella Linda was—?"

I slowly nod.

"Are you homosexual, Boyd?" There's something in his voice that's comforting, curiosity instead of the revulsion I'd expected.

"I've never thought of myself that way," I say.

"I've never thought of you that way, either. You—and the fella Linda was—?" he repeats. "How long did it go on?"

"About three months, off and on. From middle of April, after I got back in town from covering the Masters, to the Fourth of July." It still sounds like a long time to me, considering what I ended up with. "It's mostly when I'm out of town, Win. I've been discreet if I've been anything. Ed ... caught me completely by surprise."

"So you really liked the guy?"

There is perfect silence. Some things can't be admitted to, even between friends.

"When did Ed start seeing Linda? Were they—"

"Sometime in June, best I can figure. I could tell something was on his mind. Things just weren't the same between us, the last few times. Anyway, the news came over the Fourth of July weekend. I'd worked a couple hours that Saturday morning, came home to change clothes for the barbecue at the club. Phone rings. Ed tells me he'd met a woman at the Cloverleaf. Someone he was enjoying spending time with. Wanted to see where things might lead with her. Didn't even mention us."

"You and Linda were all smiles at the barbecue." Win sounds puzzled.

"We made our customary appearance."

"You mean you didn't know she was the woman Ed was seeing?"

I shake my head. "Wasn't sure till last Friday."

"Ah." Win nods. "And Ed didn't know she was married to you?"

"Not till last Friday. Being new in town, he hadn't made the connection. Not that he would have cared," I add dryly.

"Jesus." Win rubs his leathery neck. "You'd think somebody at the Cloverleaf would have filled him in."

"I don't think the two of them went to the Cloverleaf after the night they met. I don't think they went out much at all, if you get my drift."

"Help me connect the dots now, Boyd." He grasps the little finger of his left hand with the index finger of his right to make his first point. "I won't say stalking, but you were following him, weren't you? After he broke things off with you?"

"Yes."

Second point. He grasps his ring finger. "You'd seen his car in the parking lot outside a few times, next to Linda's. Couldn't stand it any longer. Had to know if he was in her apartment."

It feels good to have it out. Good to share these lonely, liquored-up summer-evening images in my head. "Yes," I say.

Third point. He grasps his middle finger. "So you got the manager, one of your fans, to give you the extra key. You let yourself in and—"

***

Linda gathers the sheet around her. Her neck is splotchy, her voice a raspy whisper. "Get the hell out!"

I take another step into the bedroom, the air heavy with the smell of sex and Ed's aftershave, which even now hits my nostrils as fresh and clean as the morning mist on the first tee at Augusta. He looks bewildered, frozen against the brass headboard, his blue eyes wide, his dark hair tousled like a little boy's. I want to cradle him, tell him everything will be okay. For I have halted their pleasure. I have accomplished what I came for. And I learn yet again that I am not good at this, at letting my feelings out, acting on them instead of tamping them back. I stand like a kid who's made the wrong entrance in the school play. I don't know what to do with my hands.

"Boyd, I mean it," Linda says, glaring at me.

Ed looks at her. He is a small man, but his shoulders are thick and strong. A wrestler's shoulders. "You know this guy?"

"This guy is her husband," I say.

He glances back and forth between us like a spectator at a tennis match. "You two are married? Linda, you told me you were—" He looks at her. "You lied to me."

"Goddammit!" She picks up one of the two sweaty glasses by the bed, hurls it at me. The thing shatters against the wall. Crown

Royal whiskey, Linda's drink of choice, spatters across my shirt. I smell its sweetness. "Get out, Boyd! Now!"

Ed is up, hunting through the tangle of clothes on the floor, and if I'm not mistaken there is a trace of amusement on his face. He's either laughing at Linda's poor shot, or the absurdity of the situation has started to settle in. Or maybe he's just plain proud of himself. "I'm the one who's leaving, Linda. I'd say the mood's been broken here." He raises his open palms to me, like he's being held up. The fact that he is totally naked, his penis shrunken between his legs, seems to make no difference at all to him. "Look, Boyd. Man. I am really sorry."

I risk it. "You didn't sound sorry on the Fourth of July."

It's Linda's turn to look bewildered. "You two know each other?"

"Sort of." Ed shoots me a warning glance.

"It meant nothing to you, Ed?" I ask.

"Sort of the beauty of it," he mutters. Ignoring me now, he picks up his shirt off the floor, puts it on, smooths his hair in place. "Give me some time, Linda, okay? You need some, too. I'll call you next week," he says to her. And surprise of surprises, he squeezes my elbow, gives it a shake as he holds it, as if to tell me everything's going to be okay. I wonder if he can smell the vodka on my breath. "See you around, Boyd?"

"Sure," I answer.

And he's out the door, leaving only a little breeze against the side of my face and the scent of his sweat. I start to follow.

"Stop." Linda pulls a small silver pistol from the drawer of the nightstand. Slams the drawer shut. Points the gun at me.

***

"She pulled a gun?" Win asks, astounded. "What the hell happened to it?"

I push myself from the doorframe, go to the brass bed. I dismantled it the other day, after the police were finished with it, and now its pieces—headboard, box springs, mattress—lean against the wall. I find the spot on the side of the mattress where I made a slit with the knife after I stabbed Linda, use my thumbnail to scrape away the stuff that covers it—Linda's blood, dried smooth and black as tar. While it was congealing, I spread it over the entry to my hiding place the way Meemaw used to spread her brown sugar icing to cover the cracks across the top of her blackberry jam cake. "No one will ever know," she would say, eyes twinkling, handing me the spatula to lick. Meemaw was right. No one will ever know. Except Win. I slide my hand deep inside the mattress, find the cool hardness of the pistol, retrieve it, present it to him in my open palms. "Ever want to hide anything …"

He recoils. "I don't want to touch it, Boyd. Put it down."

I set it on the vanity.

"Why didn't you want the police to see the damn thing?"

"Don't want them to know how she used it."

***

She keeps the gun pointed at me, drawing the sheet up a little higher over her breasts. I honestly don't know if she's bluffing or not. "I could kill you, you know?" she says.

"Get you out of my life once and for all. No one would do a goddamn thing."

"Well, Linda ..." I slap the sides of my legs. What do you say to an angry, naked woman pointing a gun at you? "If you're of a mind to do that, best go ahead and get it over with."

"And miss the pleasure of watching you sweat?"

***

Win whistles. "I knew she had a mean streak. What'd she do?"

"She asked how Ed and I knew each other, what I meant by the things I'd said to him. Having a gun on you, Win … It'll clear your head right smart. I knew telling her the truth would only provoke her—"

***

"We're friends. That's all, Linda."

She smirks. "You can fool yourself, Boyd, but you can't fool me."

Even with the crepe paper wrinkles around her eyes, she looks as pretty as Natalie Wood in her later years, a Natalie born in a trailer in Pine Level, Alabama, one who's worked pretty damn hard to escape her past. I've always respected her for that.

"Too bad your little crush is unrequited. Ed is all man." She smiles a satisfied smile as she smoothes the sheet across her lap. "He's proven it on more than one occasion."

I don't know where I'd even begin to counter that one.

"Am I free to go, Linda?"

"Ha! In your dreams!" She runs one fingernail down the length of the gun barrel. Her voice takes on a lilt as if she's reading a children's storybook. "Mama needs to teach you a lesson about chasing after her man. Mama wants to make sure it doesn't ever happen again."

She makes a little game of it. Puts her robe on one arm at a time, keeping the gun on me. She walks me out to the living room, pours more Crown Royal in the glass she didn't break.

"Get down on your knees," she says.

"Why are you doing this?"

The gun tastes like coins in my mouth. I'm not sure how serious she is. The safety is on, after all. Still, tears blur my vision. I'm thinking one more swallow of Crown Royal and she just might click the safety off and pull the trigger. So I do what she asks.

***

"God almighty." Win rubs his face with his hands. "How long does this go on?"

***

"I'll give you whatever you want in the divorce, Linda. Just—"

"Don't stop," she says to me, amused. "You're doing such a good job."

I put my lips over the barrel of the gun again, go back to the task at hand.

"You promise not to bother me, to leave Ed and me alone?"

I nod. She pulls the gun from my mouth, strokes my cheeks with it, painting them with my saliva. "There's a good boy," she says.

I've never handled a rattlesnake, but I can imagine this must be what it feels like, a cool whisper on your skin while your heart beats double-time, while you dare yourself to breathe.

The phone rings. She turns, takes the gun off me. I know it's my chance to try to wrest it from her, but my knees are stiff from kneeling, and my right leg has gone to sleep.

She goes to the phone on the wall by the refrigerator, picks up the receiver.

"Ed!"

***

"Son of a bitch," Win says, amazed. "What'd he want?"

"It sounded like the same spiel he used on me. She kept saying, 'Why? I didn't mean to lie to you, Ed.' I have to admit, my scared old heart was having a good laugh. At the same time I was cursing Ed's timing. I knew I was in deep unless—"

***

She hangs up the receiver, levels the gun at my face, steps toward me. I watch her thumb move over the safety, hear the click as she takes it off. I see, too, that her finger isn't quite in place on the trigger.

***

"You go for it?" Win asks eagerly.

"It's amazing what adrenaline can do. I spring up off these knees like a teenager, grab those skinny wrists. I surprise her. She isn't expecting me—"

"Atta boy." Win pumps his fist.

"Don't give me the trophy yet."

"She's stronger than you thought she'd be, right?"

"And hard to get a grip on. She and Ed—They'd been using a lubricant, I guess. Her hands are all slick."

***

"Oh no you don't!" she says between clenched teeth.

"Faggot—"

She breaks my grip, backs away. I grab her wrist and jerk it up so the gun points toward the ceiling.

"I will shoot you, Boyd," she hisses, twisting against me. "Just you watch!"

And there, against my right hand, is the butcher block holder for the steak knives. It's almost as if it has nudged me, a gift.

***

"She doesn't know you take the knife?" Win asks. "She misses it, in all the commotion?"

"She's spitting every name in the book at me. Somehow we get in here again. I push her onto the bed—"

***

"You goddamn—" she growls.

I plunge in the knife just below her rib cage. She draws in a breath. Her mouth makes a little o.

"Shut—" I say. I draw the knife out, plunge it in again, watch the look of surprise turn to horror. One thrust of the knife for every word boiling out of me:

"Shut. The. Fuck. Up."

***

Win pulls a folded handkerchief from his pocket, hands it to me. I wipe the sweat off my forehead. I don't know why he's grinning like the Cheshire cat.

"When did you call 911?" he asks softly.

"After I got my jealous-husband, crime-of-passion story straight. After I hid that thing." I nod toward the gun on the vanity. "The whole thing with Linda took twenty minutes, after Ed left. The police bought it. Everyone did."

"You told them what you told Linda, that you knew Ed, that you and he were friends?"

I rub my head. "It was a gamble, but I figured they'd find out eventually who lover boy was. If I'd said I didn't know him, and he told them he knew me.... Well, there goes the lid on Pandora's box. The only thing I was certain of was that Ed wouldn't tell the police any more than that we were friends, drinking buddies. It's one of the unspoken agreements between guys like us. I was right.

That's exactly what he told them." I can't resist a little laugh. "He plays the game well."

Win stands with a sigh. "Why don't you shower, Boyd? We've done enough tonight. I'll put together some sandwiches with the ham I bought, pour us some milk."

"Shouldn't you be getting home to Dottie?"

"She's got bridge at her sister's tonight. You and me, we'll sit at the kitchen table and have a regular meal. We'll celebrate."

The word is as strange as his grin earlier. "Celebrate?" I ask, folding the soft handkerchief in my hands.

He nods. "Remember what I said about being able to escape— how you've got to show you couldn't get away in order to justify killing in self-defense? It's a peculiar little twist in Alabama law, and we've met it now in spades."

This isn't at all the reaction I'd expected. "I don't care about twists in the law. The reason I confided in you was to tell you why we've got to plead. I can't go to trial and risk this getting out to ... the world. If I'd thought you'd even consider—I wouldn't have—"

"Now wait a minute," Win says, exasperated.

I try to keep my voice steady. "How bad can it be if I plead guilty to what, second-degree murder or manslaughter? Seven years at Atmore? Two off for good behavior? I'd be out at fifty-five, Win. Plenty of good years left. I bet I could even get my job back at the paper, if I'm contrite enough."

"You can't tell me you'd rather serve time! She was going to kill you! Now that I know the real story? An acquittal, Boyd. We can do it. You and me."

I hand the handkerchief back to him, my mind churning. "Ray won't ask me back if he learns the truth. You know where the fine upstanding publisher of our daily newspaper stands on the subject of—" I can't say the word. "I was in her apartment."

"You pay the rent. She was still your wife, for God's sake. You had a right." His eyes widen. "She tortured you with a gun!

And still you don't trust me." He shoves the handkerchief back in his pocket.

"Any jury in this state will have me hanging from the nearest sycamore if they find out how she used that gun on me, and why. You know that. They'll say Linda did the right thing."

"That's what you see, Boyd," he says. Then his voice drops to a whisper. He sounds like the small-town Alabama kid he was when we were in grade school. "It ain't gonna be like that."

He goes to the kitchen, leaving me alone in the bedroom, alone with my thoughts. I wonder where it comes from, Win's acceptance of what went on here. His acceptance of me, now that he knows the truth. I wonder if one of his grown boys is gay, or if he has suspicions, if that's the reason his take on all this is so different from mine.

Then I see that I am not alone, because that thing is here with me, resting on its side on the vanity, poised, quiet, watching me with its mean little eye.

I pick it up, hold it in my hands again. We became quite familiar with each other last Friday, this gun and me. You could say we're buddies, or we could be.

I raise it to my temple, let the point of it gently graze the hair on the side of my head. It tickles, the way Ed's fingers would while I—

I close my eyes. I picture sitting down to dinner with Win. Going along with what he wants me to do. Taking the gun to the DA's office tomorrow to submit it as evidence of what really went on here. It might not be so awful. Might even be—

My heart leaps as I lower the gun to my side. Might even be good? Letting people know what happened? Trusting Win to make it work? Starting a life that's better, maybe, where I could be free to—?

I catch a glimpse of myself in the gold-edged mirror behind Linda's vanity. There's my answer. I see a middle-aged man with a silly, hopeful look on his face and a gun in his hand. A man who knows better. Or should.

"Boyd," Win says, turning from the refrigerator when I set foot in the kitchen. The package of ham he's holding hits the floor with a smack.

My mind stops churning. It's quiet. Everything is clear. "There's only one way out of this, Win."

"And which way is that?" His face has gone pale.

I tell him to put his hands up, just so there's no doubt who's in control here. I wiggle the gun at him. Then I answer his question. I am Boyd Joyce, after all. Sports editor. Man's man. People expect certain things from guys like me, and I will not disappoint them.

An Overdue Parade

Micah Ward

JT McGregor ran his fishing charter boat out of the harbor at Fernandina Beach, Florida. He drank an occasional beer at Hammerheads or the Green Turtle where he would talk about the Miami Marlins or the Florida weather. Especially on days when most of the North was suffering through snow and cold while he wore a tee shirt and shorts.

JT had always been a man of the water. He spent his youth on the beaches of Amelia Island surfing and sitting by campfires watching the flames shredded by the offshore winds. He worked on a shrimp boat for a year after high school. But the war in Vietnam heated up and the draft became inevitable. As he did when faced with life altering decisions, JT sat down for a long talk with his father.

Horace McGregor was a veteran of WWII. He served on a destroyer in the north Atlantic running blockade for the merchant ships that ferried supplies from America to England. Horace suggested that joining the Navy fit with the family's tradition of going to sea. Quite a few McGregor men had served in the Merchant Marine over the years and besides, being in the Navy would keep JT out of the jungle.

"I would never tell you not to serve your country," Horace said. "But if you can cut the chances of getting killed while doing it, there's not a damn thing wrong with that."

So, just before the draft went into high gear, JT joined the Navy. After boot camp he received training in the small, fast patrol vessels known as Swift Boats. For two tours, JT McGregor rode the swift boats in shallow coastal waters and in the rivers and channels of the Mekong Delta. Suffocated in a heat and humidity that eclipsed even a Florida summer. He fired machine guns at ghostly targets who fired back. Sometimes he drove the boat, at little more than walking pace, then rocketing forward at high speed in a serpentine pattern. Incoming rounds from an ambush peppered the hull and structure. He saw sailors killed and sailors horribly wounded. He received his own scars both physical and mental.

JT brought his ghosts home to Old Town on Amelia Island. No parades. No confetti. No bands playing. A few old timers shook his hand and quietly invited him to the VFW for a beer. Former high school classmates didn't know exactly how to treat him. But at least they didn't spit on him and call him "baby killer" like that hippie in the San Francisco airport.

He went back to the shrimp boats and fought to repress the memories that rose in the early dawn. Memories triggered by smells at the marina, shifts in the wind and the motion of the shrimp boat in the channels between Amelia and Cumberland Islands. Eventually JT gained control of the memories and saved enough to buy his own fishing charter boat. His wife Katie bore them three children and JT McGregor lived a good life. And part of that good life was running his own fishing charter.

It was early on a Monday morning and the first glimpse of sunlight flowed down Centre Street and peeped over the downtown buildings to illuminate the marina. Pelicans perched on pylons and seagulls serenaded the marina as they hovered in search of food.

JT was busy preparing for the day's charter, moving from one end of the boat to the other and giving a steady stream of instructions to his new helper, Frogman. Frogman's real name was Clarence but he had been known as Frogman since the day he snuck a live frog into his 2nd grade teacher's desk drawer. It was not an exaggeration to call that the highlight of Frogman's academic career.

When the charter arrived, he was a man of about the same age as JT. He wore a Vietnam vets ball cap and walked with a noticeable limp.

"Good morning," he said as he approached the boat. "I'm Archer Brown."

"Welcome aboard," replied JT as he reached a hand out to help Archer Brown onto the boat. "We don't get many one-person parties so; you'll have our undivided attention today. This is Frogman. He'll be helping with the bait and lines and hopefully gaffing that monster fish you reel in today."

"Pleased to meet you Frogman."

JT showed Brown the coolers with water, sodas, and beer. Then the downstairs with the galley where the sandwiches were stored. The head and a bunk if needed.

A few minutes later, Frogman untied the boat from the dock and coiled the lines while JT slid the boat slowly away from the marina and into the channel toward the St. Mary's River and on to the deep water of the Atlantic. The pelicans watched sedately and the gulls whirled in circles around the boat.

As the boat turned east, JT pointed out Fort Clinch off the starboard side and gave Brown a brief history of the Civil War era fort. He then steered the boat toward the fishing areas. Frogman scurried around the boat getting fishing poles, lines and bait ready. The boat gently rode the swells into deeper water and JT began the small talk that goes with the charter business.

"I noticed on your registration that you are visiting from Kansas City. What brings you to Fernandina Beach?"

"Visiting an old Army buddy. He's been inviting me to come down here for a Shrimp Festival or some sort of thing for years.

So, I thought it was about time I took him up on it. I tried to get him to come fishing today but he says he gets too seasick. I told him to just stay home then. I don't get to fish like this very often so I wasn't going to pass it up."

"Shrimp Fest is a big deal," Frogman chimed in. "It's about as big as Christmas around here."

"Well, I'm looking forward to it. By the way, how did you get the name Frogman? Were you in the Navy?"

"Oh, no, sir. That's an old school nickname. But the captain there was Navy. He was in 'Nam too. In those little boats like John Kerry was. What did y'all call 'em captain?"

"Swift Boats," JT answered. "How are the lines coming there Frogman? We want Mr. Brown to be ready when we hit the right spot."

Brown noticed the way the captain steered the talk away from Vietnam, but let the subject drop as JT explained where they were headed and what types of fish they'd be after. He told Brown about the bait, the rods, and the habits of the fish. He explained currents, water temperatures, migration patterns and anything except small fast boats in the Mekong Delta.

It was a good day for fishing, and Archer Brown had, as he called it, a very large time. Fish were caught and fish were missed. The sandwiches disappeared and Brown put a considerable dent in the beer supply. By the end of the day the three men had become comfortable with each other and, as JT knew, that was sometimes the best thing that could occur on a fishing charter.

At the end of the day, JT eased the boat alongside the dock bathed in the soft light of sunset. Brown handed Frogman a tip of folded bills and thanked him. He turned to JT with a larger stack of bills and said, "That was a lot of fun. I really enjoyed it. Will you be in the parade with the other vets?"

"Parade?" asked JT although he knew exactly what Brown was talking about.

"Yeah, my buddy said the local Vietnam vets club will be riding a float in that Shrimp parade. I thought you might be there."

"I'm not sure," JT replied. "Depends on whether or not I have a charter."

Archer Brown departed the boat and JT watched him limp down the walkway toward the parking lot. There was no charter scheduled for Thursday. Still, JT had never ridden in the parade. He hadn't even thought about it until Archer Brown asked him.

The next morning, JT went by his father's house to check on the old man. Every morning, except on the days he ran the fishing boat, JT stopped at Horace's. It was a small house with a sandy dirt driveway, enclosed by live oak trees. A view of the marina and waterway off the porch.

"Can you believe this," shouted Horace as JT stepped into the back door. "The damned Marlins blew a four-run lead in the ninth last night. Goin' to be a long season if they keep doin' that."

JT looked at his father in his usual place in the living room. Sitting in a rocking chair by the open window absorbed by the sports page of the Jacksonville paper. JT poured a cup of coffee and sat on the sofa opposite his father. Old Horace carried on nonstop about the previous night's baseball scores. Who won, who lost, who had great performances and who stunk up the field.

Finally, the old man folded the paper and laid it on a table next to his chair.

"So, what brings you out this way?"

"Just came by to see if you were still alive."

"Yeah, I suppose you can cancel the undertaker for another day. How was the charter?"

"Kind of unusual, a one-man party. Said he was visiting an Army buddy and the buddy gets sea sick so this guy decided to fish by himself."

"Sounds reasonable."

"He's a 'Nam vet too. He and his buddy are riding in the parade with the others."

"The pirate's parade?"

"Yeah. The Vietnam Vets club is having a float again this year and a bunch of them are riding on it."

They both sat in silence until Horace asked his son, "Are you going to join 'em?"

"I don't think so. You know I never got into that kind of stuff."

The old man unfolded himself from the rocking chair and took both coffee cups into the kitchen. He refilled them and returned and handed one to his son. He stood there and stared down at JT.

"I think you should do it. We got parades when we came home. You boys got the shit stick."

The two of them eased into the comfortable silence that normally followed any talk of their wars.

On Thursday morning, JT McGregor still did not have a charter. Thursday, the day of the pirate's parade. He stood at the closet door in khaki shorts and stared at the stack of tee shirts. He could just see the dark blue edge of the one on the bottom, given to him many years before by his wife. Old but not yet faded from wear and washings. He slid it out from under the others, and unfolded it, and stared at the lettering. Simple gold letters spelled out "US Navy" and under that "Vietnam Veteran."

JT slipped the shirt on and looked at himself in the mirror. He felt slightly embarrassed. When he walked into the kitchen his wife Katie glanced at him and turned her attention back to the stove. A slight smile on her face.

She placed plates of eggs, bacon, and toast on the table and sat down without a word. She looked at him and kept smiling.

"Well?" he asked.

"I like it," she said. "Not that you wear it very often. But, I'm proud of you. You earned it."

"I think I'm going to ride in the parade today."

"Then I think I'll be there to see it."

It was early afternoon when the parade-goers began assembling in a large park at the starting point of the parade route. In the shade of the live oak trees and Spanish moss, high school bands gathered and sorted out their marching order. The local pirates' club primed the cannons on their ship float and adjusted their costumes for the best swashbuckling effect. And of course, the Shriners were there along with a few groups that appeared to be marching for no apparent reason.

JT slowly passed through the crowd. Several people smiled and nodded to him even though he had no idea who they were. Maybe it was the seldom-worn shirt. He couldn't help feeling somewhat self-conscious. He stopped when he saw them. A group of men from his generation milling about a long trailer festooned with the red, white and blue of American flags and the stark black and white POW - MIA flags. Banners reading Vietnam Vets of America stretched along the side of the trailer. Everyone around the float wore hats or shirts or both identifying themselves as Vietnam veterans. JT sighed, stood up a little straighter and walked up to the group.

"JT McGregor," exclaimed a short, stocky man in camouflage pants and a USMC shirt. "I'm glad to see you here, brother. I'm sure everyone else will be too."

JT recognized the face but couldn't pair a name with it. Others passed by with a slap on the back, a question about fishing, questions about Horace, or speculation about the chance of rain. No one told Vietnam stories and no one questioned JT about showing up for the parade. Although he knew no one expected him to be there, no one made a big deal of it either.

"Hey, Captain," said a familiar voice. "You give Frogman the day off?"

Archer Brown limped toward JT with an extended hand. Following right behind was a familiar face JT knew he had seen around town.

"This is my buddy Bill Coates," said Brown.

JT shook hands with Brown and then Bill Coates who he now recognized as a higher-up at one of the local banks. Light conversation took place among the three as others drifted by with words for Coates and welcomes for both JT and the visiting Archer Brown.

"Saddle up," shouted a voice from the trailer. JT looked up to see the short, stocky man in the USMC shirt. They all stepped up onto the trailer with varying degrees of agility, some slowed by age and some, such as Archer Brown, slowed by what they'd brought back from Vietnam.

The lead police car hit the siren and activated its lights and the caravan of floats, cars, trucks, and marching bands headed out of the park and into the streets of historic Fernandina Beach. They began that accordion effect all parades assume. The first floats stretching out and those behind accelerating to catch up then coming to a standstill before starting back into motion.

Small groups of people stood on porches and lawns of private homes cheering as the parade passed. The veteran's float was one of several sandwiched between the two marching bands. Even though the bands were several blocks apart JT smiled at the sound of the competing music from ahead and behind.

As the parade slowly moved through one intersection and on to the next, JT became more relaxed. He found himself smiling more often and actually started to wave, especially to the children.

The parade turned onto 2nd Street and the crowd began to grow. A loud cheering section at Pajama Dave's Beer Garden waved and shouted. Two women ran to the float and handed beers to outstretched hands. The vets returned the cheers of the beer garden crowd as they raised plastic cups in salute.

When the parade finally turned onto Centre Street, JT took in the shoulder to shoulder crowd that lined both sides of downtown Fernandina Beach. Many of them wore beads that he knew were being thrown from the floats and vehicles that had already passed. The children dashed on and off the sidewalks to scoop up handfuls of candy that likewise flew from the parade to the crowd.

JT smiled and waved, occasionally catching the eye of a waving onlooker. He wondered if Katie was somewhere on the parade route and if he would see her. His eyes searched back and forth from one side of the street to the other. Then, as the float approached the deck of Peppers Mexican restaurant, he heard the scream.

"JAAAAAAY TEEEEEEEE!!!"

He looked at Peppers and saw Katie standing at a table waving frantically to catch his attention. Their son and both daughters stood with her, waving and shouting. His father stood ramrod straight, his right hand to the bill of his blue US Navy ball cap. Slowly, people began to rise from their seats and applaud the Vietnam vets float. A full standing ovation.

Tears broke from JT's eyes and streamed down both cheeks. He slowly lifted his right hand and made eye contact with his father, returning the salute.

Archer Brown placed a hand on JT's shoulder and said, "Welcome home, brother."

Gnats End

Jeff Clemmons

Darlene saw the jet's vapor trails streak across the vivid azure sky as tears rolled down her cheeks and gathered like small ponds of sorrow at the base of her head, which was cratered in the bloody soil of the garden behind her house.

Her momma had told her to leave those boys alone. That they were nothing but trouble; evil bred amongst the kudzu and ignorance that swallows up Gnats End.

But what do moms know. And it was Darlene who had begged them over.

Wolves At The Door

LaVern Spencer McCarthy

Years-of-poverty-ago, a wolf
devoured our last chicken.
Crouched in a swath of blood
and feathers, fangs bared, it defied us.

Galvanized, we bolted from the woods
screeched "Murder!" all the way home.

Mama stood at the cabin door
wiping her hands on a flour sack apron,
sharing our terror. The chicken had
been planned for dinner.

I remember former chickens whose necks
Mama had wrung, her upper lip turned
downward like a beak, something reeling
in her eyes as a scrawny meal raced
its life away, out in the yard.

Before, I had managed to separate
the violence from my plate of drumsticks
and gravy, but not that night of no meat.

Shoving in collards that had not been forced
to suffer on my behalf, I watched Mama
brush a tear away as she tried to instill in us
courage to face the wolves of our days.

Best I Never Had

J. B. Hogan

You were better than the first one,
though there was no complaint,
better than those that followed
though they were hard to find,
better than the presumed one
though it really couldn't last
better than all the near ones
though they never came close
better than all the painful rest
though there had been no chance
still you were better than them all,
you were the best I never had.

Socks Come In Pairs

Fhen M.

A white-bellied robin,
active during the daytime, forages for food,
and at night, the bird sleeps.

It's like a Goldilocks planet,
with a perfect balance of day and night
a night-shift worker feels drained of energy
once daylight breaks.

Like a man who has spirit and body,
with the loss of his physical vigor,
the spark of life within him dwindles.

Amidst the chaos, life has a rhythm;
nature has time for waking and sleeping.
Time to put on shoes, and store them away.

When we lose a sock,
when we lose sleep,
when we defy nature's rhythm,
something is lost to us forever.

Davy Crockett's Trustworthy Tale of an Extraordinary Encounter With a Bear with a Bucket Who Hails from Nantucket

Ken Gosse

From the Horse's Mouth:
"This testament, written both faithful and true
by the great-great-great grandson of someone who knew
an acquaintance who heard the renowned raconteur
humbly telling his story (sans hint of grandeur).
His birthplace, a bend in the Old Nolichucky—
"The King of the Wild Frontier" from Kentucky.

The soldier, frontiersman, and statesman avowed
to the rabid attention of those in the crowd
at the inn where they gathered to listen and drink,
so attentive that not even one dared to blink
at this one-hundredth telling of such a wild tale
that it's not been surpassed by the captain's white whale.

His story:
A stare brought a bear to its knees
while the woodsman stood still, just as calm as you please.

This testament is, as I started to say,
an authentic account of his words on that day
with two verses appended, which seemed to be needed

because, as you'll see, it was never completed."
[The author's unknown and the date isn't clear,
besmudged by drunk fingers which read it each year.]

Where the Legend Began:
It was back by the old Nolichucky
where I met a huge bear who was plucky.
I froze with a stare
till he wandered from there,
and I reckoned that I was quite lucky.

How the Legend Took Root:
They say that I spoke to the bear.
To be honest, I don't really care.
What crazy suggestions—
don't ask a bear questions!
That's not how I got out of there.

How the Legend Grew:
While wand'ring our western frontier,
I heard more of my story each year—
the tale of a b'ar
who had wandered so far
from the Nantucket home he held dear.

How the Legend was Preserved:
Once I gathered each piece that I could,
I decided time spent would be good
in rehearsing the tale—
they're a great trade for ale!
Here it is, far as I've understood:

The Bucket's Gist:
There once was a bear with a bucket
who wintered outside of Nantucket.
The lair was quite bare
but a bucket was there
and a blanket, beneath which he'd tuck it.

An Innocent Beginning:
The bear took a nap on a hill,
where he frightened some poor Jack and Jill.
'Twas not his intent,
but downhill they both went,
and the bucket would need a refill.

Davy Sings the Blues:
Jack and Jill went up the hill
to fetch a pail of water.
A bear was there
and scared the pair!
They lost the pail Jack bought her.

The Best Laid Plan of Bear and Man:
A bucket and bear but no plan
(and no palindrome—search all you can).
"But what good would it do?"
"Why, of course! Hunter stew."
So he took it back home to his clan.

Strange Encounters of the Frontier Kind:
While heading back home from Kentuck,
the bear worried he'd run outta luck
and meet Davy there
who would give him "The Stare!"
then he'd say, "That's a pail, ain't it, Huck?"

The Way to a Bear's Heart:
So this big dumb ol' bear with a pail
came up with an int'resting tale
'bout a man from Nantucket
who'd just filled the bucket.
Nice snack with a chaser of ale.

A Rumor Can Outrun a Bear:
"There once was a man from Kentucket
who stared down a b'ar with a bucket.
Dave said to him, 'Smokey,
perhaps this sounds lokey:
Did you eat a man from Nantucket?"

Chug-a-Lug, Chug-a-Lug:
That's where his narration suspended—
a tad short of where he intended.
Each verse meant a slug
must be shared from a jug
till the speaker and fans were upended.

What Happened Next:
Though the answer, delectably gory,
became part of the bear's repertory,
the great storyteller
Dave Crockett, fine feller,
ne'er told us the rest of the story.

For Sale

Jeff Clemmons

The table is mahogany. Rectangular. Distressed in places. It is an unexpected find on a sidewalk outside an antique store in Darien. Six chairs, two with broken lyre backs, and a leaf. But the $150-dollar-steal is too good to pass on. Warren snatches it off the concrete and loads it onto his lopsided, busted old Ford before the salesclerk tills the money.

Within a few months, the table is stripped bare of its former history and stained and shellacked against a new one. The lyres are restrung—courtesy of his woodworking old man—and the bronze leg end caps are buffed to shine like fool's gold. An altar Warren is sure to write at. His new girlfriend thinks so, but she isn't to be trusted.

Three months past six, give or take, and Warren uses the altar for the first time. Setting his baby girl in a basket on one end, he picks up a pen and sets it to paper:

"For sale: Duncan Phyfe table, leaf and six chairs. Diapers needed. $175 OBO."

Dear Tooth Fairy

Celia Miles

To paraphrase a seventeenth metaphysical poet (can you tell I'm not your usual six-year-old correspondent?) some folks "a forward motion love, but I by backward steps would move…" into the realm, not of death, but dreams, dreams of you and Santa Claus, and Mama Nature, and all entities that create and foster the illusion of a forgiving and rational world.

Give me again the belief gleaned from wiser adults that if I am "good" (no definition required) and play by the rules, I will be rewarded. Bring me faith that if I follow a childlike path of cause and consequence, something positive will result. Give me the simple mindedness to think: If I behave thus and thus, long approved by moralists who ought to know, then surely such and such will occur.

In other words, dear tooth fairy, in case you're losing my drift, renew my expectation that something, somebody, *something* out there sees what I do and pays attention. If I risk, let's say, a tooth under my pillow, let me believe it's worth the hope. It's that faith in what's unseen that prepares a child for the growing up; it's not intellectual questioning that gets him or her ready. That comes, but its grandparent-predecessor is faith that step two follows step one.

So now, dear tooth fairy, from you I don't need a dime or a dollar. What I need is the assurance that you're there, you and all you represent. And for that I'd gladly leave you my teeth, capped and bridged as they are. After all, they can be replaced. But I'm not sure you can be.

Venus and Chenelle: A Girl's Guide to Arrival

Cindy Sams

Summer 1973

The Toronado crunched into the driveway near sunset. Our new home looked tired, like it had been washed and worn without ever being ironed. Squat, flat-roofed, mud-colored, it slouched behind a few scraggly bushes that passed for landscaping.

We'd come all the way from Macon, Georgia to Benson, Arizona that summer, dropped into the desert like stray seeds, only to face disappointment at the start.

No porch swing. No porch. Crabgrass and pigweed stood in for a lawn. In the growing dark, this house looked like all the others built on this side of town, sad and a little ashamed of itself.

We hadn't been used to anything better, but we had hoped for something different. Bobby looked at me like he didn't want to get out of the car. His eyes asked: *Is this it?*

Mine answered, *Yeah. I guess so.*

We grabbed our bags and followed the grown-ups inside, our arms full and our heads down. The screen door slammed behind us, and two poodles—Cricket and Beaumont—tore into the room, jumping and yapping like windup toys on speed. One ash-gray, one floofy black. Both out of their ever-loving minds.

Cricket peed on the floor by my new cloth suitcase, a dainty thing covered in hot pink flowers. I said nothing as the puddle spread. Someone would clean it up later, I figured.

"How do you like it?" Mama asked. Her bouffant wig sat crooked on her head, teetering to the left like it had lost all faith in Aqua Net. She pursed her lips, hands on hips, bracing for criticism.

I scanned the living room for something to compliment, but my eyes didn't know where to light first.

Mama had gone full-on 1970 with her decorating: shag carpet up to our ankles, avocado green on anything that didn't move, and a mineral oil lamp by the front door that oozed tacky charm. Inside the lamp, a statue of Venus posed like a naked hostage in a slow-drip waterfall.

She had one plastic arm raised and the other on her hip like she was about to sass somebody. The oily stuff around her two-foot form slithered up and down in golden drips. This must be what Vegas showgirls looked like, I thought. Not that I'd ever seen one, except on TV once, before Grandmama hopped up and changed the channel.

The very thought of that lamp made me blush. We didn't prance around naked like that back home. Grandmama would have called it tacky. Only hard-down, low-class folks would have something like that out front for everybody to see.

"Y'all want to see your rooms?" Mama chirped, hurrying away from the avocado fever dream she had set loose on the decorating world. I picked up my suitcase and followed her down the hall. She stopped at the first door on the right and threw it open.

The smell of fresh paint hit me square in the nose.

The walls radiated a shade of soft yellow brighter than lemon but milder than sunshine. An ivory chenille spread covered the double bed, the fabric reminding me of old lady bathrobes and crocheted doilies. Peeling laminate and cockeyed drawers told me the furniture had been bought second-hand. The window lacked curtains, but the Venetian blinds could be opened and closed against the desert heat.

This wasn't the room I'd imagined on the train, but it would be mine. A few touches from my dog-eared decorating book, and this space would belong on the cover of *Seventeen*.

"I love it." I turned to give Mama a smile, but she had already gone down the hall to Bobby's room. I wanted to ask about hanging my posters, but that could wait.

After unpacking my clothes—shorts, T-shirts, a Sunday dress or two—I sat down on the bed. A portable clock-radio on the dresser blinked the wrong time. I picked it up and set it back down, unsure about touching something I hadn't brought with me.

Voices filtered in from the kitchen. Mama fed the dogs to stop their whining. A refrigerator door opened and snapped shut. I picked at the nubby bedspread until a dime-sized hole appeared in the center. I needed a bathroom but felt too shy to go find one. Peeing on the floor seemed out of the question.

A rap against the hollow brown door. Dale asked if he could come in.

"Yes, sir."

He stood just inside the doorway and asked if I needed anything.

I stayed polite but cautious: "No, sir."

Did I like the color of my room?

"Yes, sir."

Did I want something to eat or drink?

"No, sir."

Having gotten the pleasantries out of the way, Dale got down to business.

"This is your home now," he said. "I want you to know how welcome you are here, and how glad I am you came. I hope you'll want to stay after the summer."

I kept my hands knotted in my lap. The tension made my fingers ache.

"Thank you, sir."

He left.

I cried with relief. No one had ever said they were glad to have me around. Not right out loud like that. Wiping my eyes, I lay back on the chenille bedspread and wondered what would come next. A strange shift settled in me, although nothing much had happened yet as far as I could tell.

USER MANUAL: TEMPORARY DAUGHTER

Model: Pre-Owned | Series: June 1973 | Issued by: Maternal Transfer Authority

Congratulations on acquiring your new daughter. While not factory-issued, this model has been previously housebroken by maternal grandmother and displays mild obedience when properly motivated. Please read the following instructions carefully for optimal performance:

1. Do not feed after dinner. Weight gain voids the warranty.
2. Praise reading habits occasionally. No more than once per month.
3. Limit emotional displays—except when guests are present, in which case the model should perform affection on command.
4. Voice settings: Southern drawl must be adjusted to neutral or "TV English" when in public.
5. Maintenance tip: Apply White Shoulders perfume to simulate comfort and familiarity.
6. Never acknowledge pre-owned condition or prior attachments. Especially not to Grandmama.
7. Store out of direct light. This model is not designed to shine.

The summer deepened along with the heat. Our suitcases got shoved deep in the back of our closets.

Back home in Macon, summer heat felt wet as a wrung-out towel slung over your head. You could suffocate standing on your own front stoop. Here, folks made a big deal about the temperatures hitting 110 degrees in the shade.

I didn't get what the big deal was about. The weather was sharp, but at least I could breathe.

It was the first time I knew that heat and families could come in more than one kind. Wet vs dry. Georgia vs Arizona. Mama vs. Grandmama. One swamped you. The other dried you out. Neither let you come up for air without a cost.

I wondered what my friends back home were doing without me. Was Cynthia at the piano or getting ready for another violin lesson? She could play any instrument she picked up.

All I could handle was the FM radio. I reached over and turned it on, trying to drown out the noise of the life I'd left behind.

Bobby made friends at the local pool. I checked out books at the library and considered those my companions.

The librarian always gave my selections the side-eye: *The Story of My Life* by Helen Keller. *A Patch of Blue* by Elizabeth Kata. *The Odessa File* by Frederick Forsyth.

"These are a little advanced for you, aren't they?" she asked.

"They're not as hard as *Anna Karenina*," I said. "I read that in the fifth grade. I'm going to the eighth now."

The librarian frowned, stamped my books, and waved me on.

What was her problem? Nobody had ever cared if I read above my grade level. That was one of the few things I was ever praised for.

Mail call.

A letter from Cynthia arrived covered in her usual doodles. Among them: her version of crazy Anthony's famous flailing arm, fist raised like he was about to slap the dog-mess out of someone or ask to use the bathroom.

She drew those cartoons right on the envelope, alongside a fair picture of our teacher Mrs. Blackburn's loopy permanent wave. Those scribbles were important. They were a secret code that kept our thoughts safe from prying eyes.

Inside the letter, Cynthia wrote about the latest doings at her house: sister Amelia's new Sunday dress, the giant zit on her own nose, the morning paper route she ran with her daddy.

"I fell asleep in the car delivering papers again. I think we need a later route." She always dozed off during their morning chore. I'd filled in for her lots of times when I spent the night over at her house.

The letters made me feel more *there* than *here*, like I could still be a part of my old life while living so far away. We shared a name and a whole lot more than that. We were best buddies in a world where friendship was hard to hold onto at any distance.

I wrote back right away. "Cricket is such a wimp. That dog pees all over the house and trembles like a stick if you look at her … my brother's room has a black light … the weather is so hot … there's not a lot to do …"

Layers of squiggles covered my return envelope. Anthony's arm, our sixth-grade teacher's hairdo, Cricket shivering in a corner. Mama made me stuff the whole thing into a bigger envelope so the pictures wouldn't show.

than I let on. Cynthia's letters were the one thing that summer that made me feel like myself.

Everything about me embarrassed Mama: my weight, my accent, even my mail. I stopped drawing on envelopes. I used "you all" instead of "y'all." I chewed the Ayds diet candies she said would curb my appetite.

They didn't.

Little by little, I shrank myself from the inside out. If I got small enough, she'd be proud of me. But the smaller I got, the more invisible I became.

Transformation

Robin Prince Monroe

It was only out in the farthest upper pasture that fifteen-year-old Emrys could let go and run. When he ran full-out his mind went into a hypnotic flow and the earth could no longer hold him down. Once he lifted off he was no longer aware of the fiery sunshine on his face, or the force of the wind brushing back his wavy, auburn hair. His mind went somewhere else entirely. Only his little, fuzzy, white dog, Zephyr, could bring him out of the trance that gave him so much joy.

Actually, Zephyr, was not a dog at all… well by earth standards he was. He looked like a dog, sounded like a dog, and when around humans, acted exactly like a dog. But in reality Zephyr was Emrys' guardian, his best friend, and part of an elite force of the Royal Watch from their home planet, Lumin. Zephyr was commissioned to keep Emrys safe and on track, and that was a big charge for such a little nondog.

Emrys and Zephyr snuck out of the house earlier than usual because Mrs. Driscoll had gone to the grocery store, a chore that would take her most of the day since they lived so far out in the country. Mr. Driscoll was at an auction in a nearby county hoping to pick up a couple of piglets and some chicks to add to the coop population that had dwindled in the past month. He had no idea why his chickens kept disappearing. It quite upset him. So before he left early that morning, he'd taken great care to shore up the fence hoping to solve the problem.

It was a bright summer day with a light breeze out of the north perfect for letting go. And with Zephyr at his side that's exactly what Emrys did. He let go and ran. As he gathered speed he could feel the tall grass swishing across his legs, and the damp ground cool on the bottom of his tough, bare feet. The air smelled of dirt, rain, and sunshine, but when he rose high above the lacy summer clouds its aroma changed to the sweet freshness of star dust.

"Hold back, Emrys!", Zephyr's normally sing-song voice was gruff since he had become a dog. He growled it out, "Hold back, boy! It's not time."

Emrys whole body vibrated when he neared transformation speed. It was almost impossible for him to hold back when that happened, but he had to. There were so many depending on it, and many more who didn't know they were depending on it. He couldn't let go. Not yet.

The only way he could hold back was to start thinking about earthly responsibilities; education, farm chores, and the fate of mankind. By the time his mind got to farm chores he was no longer above the clouds and when the weight of mankind's fate came to mind he'd have crashed down if he hadn't been holding on to Zephyr.

They just made it. Emrys had gotten home and had finished feeding the last of the barn animals when his parents arrived. Mrs. Driscoll pulled her Rambler in first, with Mr. Driscoll in his ancient, green truck close behind.

For all intents and purposes the sweet couple had become Emrys' parents when they found him in the same field from which he and Zephyr had just returned. He was a tiny newborn when Mrs. Driscoll heard him mewing in the tall grass. When she went over to see what she had heard, she found him tucked in a seagrass basket and wrapped in a silver blanket. Zephyr was standing over him staring up at her with a penetrating stare.

They never talked about it, not even once, but somehow they knew that he was their long-awaited son, and that the furry, white dog was part of the package. They never talked about it, when in the middle of the night they heard a tiny giggle and found him reaching up for the stars that twinkled through the skylight above his crib. They never talked about it, when at only seven months old, he stood up one day and ran across the room, having never walked or even crawled. They never talked about the fact that each morning when Emrys woke up his eyes were a bright aqua-blue and by the time he went to bed they'd be so dark that they were almost black. They never talked about any of it. They just loved. They loved this beautiful, strange child and they loved him with all their hearts. A gift, a blessing, were the words they used when others commented on their lovely fair skinned boy with otherworldly eyes.

In just over a week Emrys would turn sixteen. The Driscolls weren't exactly sure when his birthday was, so they chose to celebrate it on the date they had found him, April 22.

He never had many friends. He had been verbally bullied most of his short school life. He'd probably have been physically attacked too if it weren't for Zephyr and his mighty growl. Anyway, he'd already learned all that school had to teach him. So he stayed home and continued to study by reading everything he could get his hands on.

Emrys did, however, manage to find one friend. Danica and her mom lived in the woods in a small, pink house that was down a dirt trail not far from the upper pasture. Danica had been bullied at school too, so she was homeschooled now.

Emrys discovered Danica one day when he was heading home after a practice flight. Fourteen and tiny for her age, he spotted her curly, blonde head in the distance. When he moved closer he could hear her tinkling laugh and was immediately drawn to the shy smile that reminded him of the starlight that he loved so much. Emrys and Danica had both spent most of their growing up safely tucked away and alone except for their animal friends, Zephyr and Silverbird, Danica's noisy pet bird.

The Driscolls usually celebrated quietly, just the three of them. But they wanted Emrys' sixteenth to be special, so they invited Danica and her mom down for a picnic and some birthday punch. Zephyr wasn't happy about that. April 22, Earth Day, was the very day of Emrys' transformation. Emrys insisted that a celebration was exactly what he needed before flying into… who knows what… for what reason?

He knew deep down in his heart of hearts, that he had to make the giant leap into Transformation. And he knew, as well as he knew the stars, that if he didn't, it would be disastrous. But he didn't know exactly what was going to happen, and Zephyr either couldn't tell him, or didn't know himself. All Emrys knew was what Zepher had told him. Lumin and Earth were connected, had always been connected. Like twins who can feel each other's pain the two planets felt the best and the worst of the other, and Earth was in a murky place right now. Truth had become difficult to find on Earth but like stubborn glitter it gleamed in the muddy mess, and as long as it did there was hope.

Earth's gray air hovered above oceans full of plastic and poison. The minds of most humans were filled with the garbage of confusion and division, and their hearts were smudged with charcoaled hate. And all of this darkness was dimming the light of Lumin. The twin planets were depending on Emrys' flight to bring light.

The week before his birthday Emrys and Zephyr were feverishly working on a plan to get Emrys to the field at just the right moment. And they were making practice flights every time they had a chance to slip away. What they didn't know is that Danica's mom sat in her attic window watching and making plans of her own.

When the day finally came, Emrys and Zephyr were confident about the adventure ahead and relieved that their purpose would finally be realized. All they had to do now was get through this dinner, wait for the Driscolls to settle into their books, then go out to do the evening feed. Everything was ready for the transformation flight. The atoms of earth were trembling in anticipation.

Danica and her mom, Lilith, arrived at the Driscoll's farm with a basket full of bread, a flask full of berry wine, and a fresh apple pie. Emrys' parents welcomed them at a weather-worn, outside table.

Mrs. Driscoll ladled beef stew into her best blue and white bowls and passed them around. They each tore a piece of the dark bread that Lilith had baked and slathered it with freshly churned butter. The adults talked of birthdays they remembered, and of happier times. Danica and Emrys were chatting quietly too, while Silverbird and Zephyr eyed each other under the table. They finished the meal with a slice of the delicious apple pie. All except Lilith who claimed she didn't have a spec of room for it.

By the time dusk settled over the group they had fallen into a deep sleep. All except Lilith, and Zephyr who had realized too late what was happening. He was feigning sleep until he could decide what to do.

When Lilith believed that they were all immobilized she stood up, ran across the yard to the field, and flew up into the sky. A sooty smoke emanated from her. It filled the air with an odious stench and covered the ground with ashes.

It's all over, Zephyr said to himself. Emrys transformation time has come and gone. Lilith brought the transformation of darkness. Earth and Lumin are forever shadowed.

They slugged through the rest of summer. Danica stayed at the Driscoll farm, the only mom she ever knew had apparently abandoned her. Fall came in hard, threatening a long, cold winter. Zephyr grew older and grumpier. The farm was failing. There was little to feed the animals and less to eat since dark clouds constantly covered the sun. A heavy sadness and tired spirit hung in the air squeezing out all joy. Emrys escaped the new darkness by climbing into his books after he finished his chores. His friends and family worried as he pulled further and further away from them for worlds that words sketched in his mind. But the end of September brought a few weeks of Indian summer and with the warmth came, for Emrys, a renewed desire to fly.

He wasn't sure he could anymore, and he was pretty certain Zephyr had grown too old to steady him back to earth. So even if he managed to get up into the air it was more than likely he would crash back down. The most compelling reason not to try was that the whole purpose of it had been thwarted. But he couldn't shake it. The books were no longer enough to hide from the darkness that was smothering him. Soar or crash he had to try.

On the evening of September 29 Emrys slipped out the back door leaving Zephyr sleeping on the hearth and Danica in the kitchen helping Mrs. Driscoll clean up after their meager supper of bread and tomato gravy. What he didn't know was that Silverbird was watching.

Emrys' step lightened as he tread up the rocky road to the upper pasture. He had missed flying. He needed to breathe the sweet stardust air above the pewter clouds that now always covered the sky.

Just one more corner and he'd be there. He could hardly wait. When he came around that last bend Lilith was there waiting for him. He could tell it was Lilith, but she had become obese with greed. A blanket of dank, angry hate covered her like sticky molasses. Her once lovely smile had become a frozen snarl.

"Stop! Stop right there! Right now!" Her voice rasped out of her plump, chapped lips.

"Why do you care what I do? You have already won."

But Lilith stood tall and fat blocking the way. When Emrys tried to go around her she drew a giant knitting needle from her sleeve and lunged for him, aiming for his heart. Just as he was about to be pierced, Zephyr, Silverbird, and Danica appeared out of nowhere and jumped Lilith knocking the giant needle away and pushing her down the steep road. She rolled to the bottom of the hill, her crash echoing with a thud.

With only a nod of thanks, and a new urgency that he didn't understand, Emrys ran the rest of the way up the road. His friends followed. When together they finally reached the pasture, he turned to them and asked, "Why? Why did you come to help me after I had let you all down?"

Zephyr answered with one word, "Hope".

Emrys' eyes filled with tears as he looked back one last time. Then he turned and ran full-out across the field.

And he let go.

When he did he rocketed up. His head shattered the ashen sky. Glitters of light fell around him like snow, and a rainbow exploded over the world.

Then iridescence returned to Lumin. Brilliant color painted the Earth. And a bath of truth illuminated the universe.

Emrys never returned. He could no longer hold back. Instead, he flew from planet to planet eating up the darkness, transforming it to light.

He had finally, completely, joyfully, let go.

County Fair 1962

Beverly Fisher

Staggering through moldy stables
In 100-degree heat to gawk
At an infinity of monstrous cucumbers, acrobatic
squash, Various deformed vegetables and miserable
livestock Unaware of their blue-ribbon glory.

Well-worn bleached blondes in two-sizes-too-small
Laura Petrie capri pants
Luring men into a dark tent with hoochie coochie come-hithers, and
Unshaven, toothless men taking
Precious quarters for rigged shooting galleries,
Over-rated *freaks,* gagging cotton candy, shaky spook houses, and
Repetitious rides delivering regurgitating fun.

Daddy, can we go again?

Bellum Civile

Rickie Zayne Ashby

Scars created by a storm
The moon dripped blood
Horsemen in grey filled the sky
Martyrs statues arose
From the ashes the future appeared
Like the Phoenix from the past

Delusions abound
Flags of white linen
Oppression once more
Celebrating a lost cause
Chasing elusive dreams
Ignoring the truth

Emerging clouds darken the sky
Pain, poverty and violence once more
Elitist waver over the abyss
Reality rejected
Crucified on a flaming cross
Peace in the valley
--Eternally denied.

Vilulah

Jeff Clemmons

It was the way in which my grandmother held her head that I learned sorrow; it was in her home that I learned salvation. I knew neither of these things when I shot her. And when Momma found me with the gun, she whispered, "Can't miss things you never had."

She Never Knew Where She Wanted To Be

Maria Mackas

"I want to go home," she'd say, whether she was in Georgia, where she lived for more than seventy years, or Cyprus, where she was born. It was the one constant in my mother's life, the one thing you could count on; she wanted to go home. But where was home? She was never sure.

Long before Alzheimer's stole her from us, she said she wanted her ashes taken to Cyprus and spread in the Mediterranean. I promised I would make it happen.

So when I found myself stranded on a train in Italy with her ashes in a Tupperware container, it wasn't really surprising that, inexplicably, the train stopped for an hour and a half, midway between Tarantola-Cortona and Rome, where I was heading to catch a flight to Larnaca, Cyprus. Again, she was caught in between. I missed my flight, spent the night in Rome and bought a ticket for the next flight, which was the next day. I was pissed. And exhausted.

But after thinking about it, it was so her. She never could decide where the hell to be. Every vacation to the beach, as our family of five packed into the un-airconditioned behemoth of a Mercury for our eight-hour drive, she would announce, "I'm not going," and march back into our split-level Tucker home (also un-airconditioned – this was the 1960s). My brother and I and grandmother were so accustomed to it, we just sat in the car with the windows rolled down and amused ourselves for the 15 minutes or so it took Papa to cajole her back out. They must have argued or something—who knows. It was hard to keep track of her back-and-forth nature.

And incomprehensible. Until I learned her duality was not uncommon among immigrants. I spent five years studying immigrant literature as I worked toward my doctorate in Literary Studies at Georgia State University. Literature had always been a solace; growing up in an immigrant family, books were where I turned when I was called nigger or hairy or repeatedly asked where I was from. Immersing myself in *Little Women* by Louisa May Alcott or *Heaven to Betsy* by Maud Hart Lovelace, where people were good and kind to others, and Jo and Betsy dreamed of being writers, helped me escape. Now literature provided comfort in a bigger, epiphanic way – revealing truth. My dissertation focused on four books with ties to Georgia immigrants; I interviewed seventeen immigrants to Georgia and juxtaposed their stories to those in the two novels and two memoirs. The common themes were uncanny: prejudice, hybridity, the struggle to assimilate, reluctance to denounce native citizenship, to name just a few. The immigrants, from places as varied as Nigeria and Ireland, had experiences that closely mirrored those of immigrants in the literature. And those of my mother.

Researched and written during the first Trump administration, my dissertation captures the fears and anxieties of first- and second-generation immigrants during those years. And the anxiety brought on by those emboldened to voice what was always right below the surface: racism.

There was also that universal truth that if you looked different or had an accent, you had to prove yourself more worthy. My mother wanted me to be perfect; an "A" wasn't good enough; "A+" was better. Fuzz on your face was unacceptable, even when you're ten years old; regular, painful waxing made you look more American. Friends were not to be trusted; you were just a runner-up for Miss Tucker High School because your jealous friend in charge of counting the votes stuffed the ballot box.

My mother was complicated, conflicted, confounding. My father drove her crazy. Yet when I took her to New York for a long weekend I was awakened to her voice from the bathroom where she pulled the phone to longingly talk to my dad: "She's dragging me everywhere. I miss you, Jimmy." When she finally achieved her dream of buying a flat in Cyprus (no small feat – my mother was a secretary, my father a waiter) what did she do but sell it after only a few years because she couldn't stand the smell of the Turkish neighbors' cooking. You'd think that when my husband and I decided to adopt a baby from Guatemala, my mother would be accepting of a child from another culture. But she warned us not to expect her to love a child "not of her blood." Then she laid eyes on our little one and everything changed. They became soulmates and she once revealed, "I loved you, but nothing like I love Marra." Hurtful? Actually, it made my heart sing. I reveled in their bond. It was one of the only times I felt my mother experienced pure joy.

When I told Marra I planned to spread my mother's ashes in Cyprus, she said she'd meet me there. I was in Italy with my husband, celebrating the completion of my PhD. Marra was living in England with her fiancé. Together, we had spread some of my mother's ashes in the Gulf of Mexico, on the Florida beach where I had vacationed with my family as a child, and where, years later, we would all vacation together. I had also spread some in the North Georgia creek that bordered our cabin property. More than twenty years earlier, we had spread my father's ashes there. She loved the mountains, the ocean, Georgia—and Cyprus.

Marra and I waded into the Mediterranean one beautiful April morning and tossed my mother's ashes into the clear, cool water. It was curious: They lingered on the surface. Then they settled on the bottom in a clearly discernible shape. I blinked and stared at what I saw. Was I creating my own kumbaya moment? I looked at Marra just as she said, “Oh my God. It’s a star.” Star—one of Marra’s first words, uttered softly as she watched *The Lion King*. “Marra’s Star” was a story I wrote for her right after we brought her home. I had just given Marra star earrings from Italy. We had just talked about getting matching star tattoos.

I’d like to believe my mother was finally at peace and was sending us a message. She was finally happy. She was everywhere all at once.

A Dilapidated Kingdom

Jim Cherry

I surveyed my empery; it had become a dilapidated kingdom. The house had fallen into disrepair; it became a symbol in my mind of the decadent state I found myself in. I noticed some of the slats on the roof had loosened and were sliding off. My father had stopped coming to the cabin when the trip had become too much for him. What had once been a bare patch of dirt that was created by tons of cars sitting over it for years, tires spinning out, oil, petrol, and every kind of viscous fluid it takes to run a car had made it a barren spot. The grasses had grown in, healing the scars of our intrusions.

Inside the dusty ruins, the air smelled musty from not having the doors or windows opened in years. Everything looked pretty much as I remembered it, although the furniture was covered with sheets, it was the ruins of a life; this was my true inheritance; I was the inheritor of lost generations before me.

I spent the next few days cleaning up the place, taking the sheets off the furniture, throwing open the doors and windows, getting fresh air back into the place, and sweeping out the cabin. I got the power and the water back on. No one had informed the utility companies of my father's death, and his accounts were still good so I reactivated them, so I would have the basic utilities until they sent out the bills and discovered my father was dead.

They say your taste in music solidifies when you're about thirty, an ossifying of your soul before the final transformation.

The last iteration of rock and roll to come along was Grunge. A band from America, Nirvana, a state which they seemed to have attained with Lithium. I wondered how I could get to that state and learn to forget. U2 and their *Joshua Tree* album which pretty much summed up what I had experienced, and The Screaming Trees *Butterfly*, more nihilist and lacking hope than previous iterations of rock. It was the soundtrack I listened to as I cleaned the cabin. It was the last kind of music I liked.

I took long rambling walks through the field and around the lake, it was a true respite from the world. I didn't have to be anywhere; I didn't have to do anything or be anyone. I felt free, I felt like I was restoring myself, that I was regaining a sense of myself. I felt like I was making peace with the ghosts that me and my father had left behind. I decided to put the Mauser back in my father's rifle cabinet, back in its place of honor, gone now was the ceremony and pomp.

After the whole house was cleaned, I decided to give myself a break and relax, sitting around drinking beer and making myself grand meals with food from the town, again on my father's accounts.

Despite all the cleaning I had done, there was still one last room to go through. A room I don't think I had even been in since I was a teenager, it was the room I never dared to go into except by 'invitation' of my father. The room I was dreading going into, his study. It had been almost a year since he'd died. All his major papers had been at the family house, but there was still his desk here that I hadn't yet gone through. The room was sealed like an ancient Pharoah's tomb or a room that held some horror behind its sealed door. Would there be treasures or just an ancient stone sarcophagus of memories?

Maybe that's why I had been so industrious the last few days with the other chores, to avoid this room and what lay inside. But the chores were done, and there was nothing else left to do, no more excuses to avoid it. I walked up the stairs as silently and stealthily as if my father was still up there and could come out of the room at any moment and ask what I was doing in that accusatory tone he had. I hadn't liked coming up here when I was a kid, there was nothing of interest to me in that room. Any time I was 'invited' into my father's study was usually for some sort of 'disciplinary matters,' as he called them. It was the opposite of telling someone they could go into any room of the house except one, I knew what monster had lurked behind that door. I kept my eye on the door the whole time I was walking up the stairs. Finally, I stood in front of the door, I hesitated, gathering my courage, I reached my hand out, it was shaking, I couldn't do it.

In the next few days, the fear of what lay behind the door grew exponentially in my mind, until wild chthonic horrors resided behind that closed door. Finally, I couldn't put it off any longer. I went up the stairs, grabbed the doorknob, turned it and pushed. It squeaked open like it was out of a haunted house. I made a final push into the room; it was as dry and desiccated as a Pharoh's tomb. There was nothing behind the door except what was supposed to be there, my father's law books, filing cabinets and his desk. The room smelled musty, stale, but different than the rest of the house. It was the smell of aging paper that I had always associated with my father. In a confined space like this it was quickly making me nauseous. I pulled open the wooden shutters that covered the large windows that looked out at the field, the woods, and the nearby lake. The room was filled with more light than it had been in a long time. My father had liked to open the windows to let the fresh air in and listen to the birds. I pulled the sheets off the chair and the desk and sat down. My father's desk wasn't all that big or impressive looking, it was stained a natural brown color and only had seven drawers. Three on either side and one long one that ran horizontally across the top of the desk, and there was the piece my father put in after I had accidentally started that corner of the desk on fire when I was ten.

I spent the afternoon going through the desk, most of the papers I found were trivial notes to himself on a case or something he had just put in his desk as a curio. When I opened the next drawer there was a Polaroid paper clipped to a couple of other papers. The picture on top was of the three of us, my mother, father, and me, in front of the cabin, it was taken when we first got it. I remembered taking the picture, but now the blue of the sky was fading, the edges were brown and yellowing to a sepia tone, the colour of nostalgia. I smiled at seeing the picture. I remember being happy when the picture had been taken, and my parents were happy too. Maybe this was our last happy moment before everything had happened, before everything had turned into a war. I remembered being that kid. I remembered me, it was like life was becoming a remembered act, we remember being happy, instead of recognizing the moment for what it is and experiencing it.

I remember running around in the grass before being gathered up for the photo. I could see pieces of me in both of them, not just a physical resemblance but pieces of their personalities as well, both my father and mother reside within me like broken pieces of a jigsaw puzzle refitted to form me. My father's assuredness and confidence in himself and my mother's ambitions and restiveness. These were the forces warring within me, a war that is never over when it's you, when it's your life. He, me, was looking back at me from the picture and I wondered what he would think of me now. I looked into the eyes of the boy in the picture.

"Do you know me, or did I kill you off too?"

I wished I could go back to that time before we became what we were now. Maybe if I concentrated enough, I could send myself back there through some act of will. In my mind I could almost reach out and touch it, I was there. I opened my eyes, and I was still holding the picture, looking into the past, and it was gone, back in time, where it belonged, and I was back where I was at.

Under the picture was a folded piece of paper, I unfolded it and read it. I wasn't expecting it; it was out of context of what had come before. It was my mother's death certificate, and it was dated a few days after I won the Olympics. The bastard had lied to me! My father had said my mother had died before the Olympics, and he made it sound like it was a long time before, and then he had the nerve to blame me! He didn't even have the courtesy to tell me when she had really died. My father was nothing more than a cog in the machine state who used their tactics and rationale to manipulate people, including his own son! Whatever he had thought of my 'antics' as he called them, I never tried to manipulate others for my gain. He probably had used my talent to leverage whatever he wanted from the state. I wondered if my mother had seen me win at the Olympics. Did she hold out to see me win and then let go? My father had even denied me the knowledge of what my mother thought of me. The bastard!

The next folded paper was even more out of context than the last. It was a letter from my mother, I could hear her voice in the words, a voice I hadn't heard in a long time. As I read farther into the letter a tear rolled down my cheek.

a nurse tricked me, she asked me how I would kill myself if I could, when I answered the question, the question they asked, they locked me in a cell because I was suicidal. I was distraught, there was another woman in the cell, and she was comforting, and we ended up having sex.

I couldn't read any more of the letter. I cried for the deception, the betrayal my mother had suffered at the hand of my father, her husband, he was the state, he was the institution. I had been right; betrayal is the hallmark of their empire. I couldn't figure out what had possessed him to paper clip these three things together, what did he think they had in common? The only thing I could figure out they had in common was my mother. I searched through my father's desk looking to see if there were any more letters from my mother. There weren't. Is this all he thought of her, these three items? I looked at the letter from my mother, it was undated. Was it one of the first letters she sent him? Or one of the last? I couldn't tell, it was obviously aged, it had been in my father's desk for a long time. Was he keeping it as some sort of trophy? Some victory over her? Or was it some source of regret or even guilt about what he'd done to her? Did he cry over the letter, or did he feel vindicated? Did the letter confirm her instability to him? I didn't know my father. I couldn't even guess which was the right answer to any of the questions.

Do Unto Others

LaVern Spencer McCarthy

At first, Benton paid no attention to the ads in the tabloid. Those found at the checkout station of a grocery store held little interest for him. He looked at the front of the paper, known for its shock value and marveled that it showed a woman who supposedly had fifteen babies within the space of twelve hours.

A spaceship sat in someone's yard on the second page. The headline stated: I play golf with aliens! On the back page were the usual requests for pen pals from prisons around the country. Benton grimaced. *No, thank you, he said to himself. Anyone who wrote those bozos would be asking for trouble.*

His wife, Irma, had returned from grocery shopping less than an hour before, spending most of his paycheck for her purchases. This trashy paper was another one of her ways to waste money. She had piled her cart high with snacks, especially the chocolates she gobbled by the box.

Benton and Irma had not gotten along with each other for years. Lately, they were at each others' throats almost daily. Benton was afraid they would physically fight or at least give each other a resounding slap. So far, he had restrained himself, but knew one day his temper might snap.

Benton was stuck at a dead-end job at a donut factory, and Irma never let him forget it. He left his dirty clothes on the bathroom floor just to irritate her. He filled his ashtray with cigarette butts and then dumped them on the floor when he needed a clean ashtray. He piled dishes on the coffee table instead of taking them to the kitchen when he was finished eating.

Irma did her part by only washing dishes when it was time to make another meal. She favored take-out meals. She loved to sit on the sofa and eat chocolates while watching soap operas.

Benton was so disgusted he found a waitress to flirt with. He hoped it would lead to a wild romance to relieve his impossibly dull life. He glanced at the tabloid again. This time he saw an ad almost at the bottom of the page. *Are you having a problem with your significant other? Is someone you know driving you crazy? Have you often thought there was no way out, that you are doomed to be stuck with this person for life? We have a foolproof way for you to get rid of your nuisance. Please email us at h&penterprises.com.*

Hmm, Benton thought. Maybe he would give it a try.

He glanced at Irma, sitting on the sofa, her eyes glued to the television screen. A chocolate bonbon was halfway to her open mouth. If things didn't change soon, he might email that company and see if they could help them.

Irma and Benton had no children, for which he was thankful. Irma had stopped mentioning children after being stuck for three weeks babysitting a squally two-year-old niece whose nose ran all the time. The niece's mother had been in a car accident, and it took a while for her to heal and take possession of her child again. Benton could escape by going to work part of the time, but Irma bore the brunt of taking care of the child. She did her part, but she was glad when the mother came for the brat.

Benton was especially glad there were no children to worry about, three days later when he decided to act. One of Irma's friends had seen Benton kissing that luscious waitress over the counter at her workplace. Of course, the dirty spy wasted no time getting to a phone to blab on Benton.

Irma was waiting for him at home. She threw a pan of hot water at him when he came through the door. Fortunately, it missed him, but Irma was on such a tear, she threw everything at him she could get her hands on. He ended up with a mound of butter stuck to his forehead. He was glad she did not throw the computer at him in her rage.

That night after she had gone to bed, Benton typed in the email address he had seen in the paper. He was able to set up a date and time to meet a Mr. Shipley.

Shipley was a cadaverous man, over six-feet tall. He had greasy, gray hair that likely hadn't seen a barber in six months. He had a large hump on his back that made Benton think of a turtle. He looked at Benton as they sat across each other at the Dixie Land Café, about thirty miles from where Benton lived.

Shipley had a black case with him that he put on the table. Undoing the latches, he withdrew a contract.

"You must understand that although this program is funded by the US Government, if state or federal law finds us to be kidnappers, we could be in jail for many years. You must promise not to tell a soul anything about H&P Enterprises."

"I won't," Benton promised, picking at his chef salad.

"Very well then," replied Mr. Shipley. "Who are we talking about that you want to get rid of?"

"It's my wife, Irma. She's driving me crazy."

"That's usually the case," Mr. Shipley agreed. "Your wife will be living in a space capsule that will orbit the earth for thirty years. How old is your wife?"

"She's thirty-one," Benton told him

"That's a good age," Shipley replied. "If she survives her ordeal, she will still be young enough to enjoy life when she is set free. Meanwhile, you can go about your own life, even have her declared dead after seven years. There will be very little for her to do once she is imprisoned. However, each day she must type something on a computer that is hooked up to the Government Studies System. It is a program to enable the government to find out how humans react to very little sensory stimulation. Of course, she does not have to record her thoughts every day, but if she does not, her food supply will stop. Her meals will be fortified with vitamins and minerals. About once-a-week real food will be added to her supply. It will be on board when she is catapulted into space. Oxygen tablets will be provided. They will be automatically fed into a processor to keep fresh air flowing for the duration of her stay."

Shipley withdrew a pen from his shirt pocket. He showed Benton where to write his wife's name, which was Irma Zipp. Benton signed on the dotted line and agreed to pay H&P enterprises a small sum of two hundred dollars for processing,

After being told that food would be forthcoming on the capsule by punching in a menu on an apparatus that resembled a microwave oven, Benton handed over the money in cash. Shipley wrote a receipt for services rendered. The men shook hands and left the restaurant.

Shipley had given Benton drugs to put into Irma's drink, and a date and time had been set for her abduction. It was suggested that a door be left unlocked on the fateful night. Benton touched the vial in his pocket. At last, he would be free.

On the night Irma Was to meet her fate, she and Benton ignored each other as they sat in the living room watching television. Irma had poured herself a glass of tea, but Benton had to get his own. Irma had not spoken to him for days, but that was fine with him. He could barely contain himself at the thought that Irma would be leaving soon.

He saw his chance when Irma went to the bathroom, leaving her drink on the coffee table. He swiftly emptied the vial of powder into her tea, swished it around with his finger and returned to the sofa where he had been sitting.

Strangely, when she returned, Irma seemed to be avoiding her tea. He watched her furtively for a while but soon relaxed a little and closed his eyes. He slept, then stirred himself and took a big swallow of his tea. Irma was gone, but her glass was empty. Benton smiled. The deed was done.

Thinking how wonderful life was going to be, Benton drifted back to sleep. Sometime later, he jerked awake from a deep slumber. He was groggy and disoriented. Where was he? Things did not feel right, and he heard a low, humming sound coming from somewhere.

He was lying on a hard surface on his side. A shoe with a foot in it was almost against his right eye. Slowly he sat up, rubbing his head. He raised his eyes and looked directly into the face of Irma.

"What the…?" he started to say when a wave of dizziness hit him.

"You've been drugged," Irma said. "We drugged each other. I put drugs in your tea while you were sleeping." The awful truth began to dawn on Benton.

"Where are we?" he croaked.

"We are in a capsule going around the earth. I was told by a message left here on paper that it would be in orbit for about thirty years, plenty of time for us to lose our sanity."

"So, you had me put here the same way I did you, without knowing you would be trapped here too?" he accused.

"Yep, that was the way it happened."

"I could kill you," he threatened.

"I wouldn't if I were you," she advised. "You wouldn't want to be stuck here with a dead body for thirty years."

Benzo Brain

Martha Ellen Johnson

Benzo Brain #1
[Lost.]

"It's a chemical imbalance
in the brain." Ad copy from
Don Draper. I bought it. An
almost mouse scampers
across the floor. A Native
woman with saucer eyes.
She's nice. Someone in the
kitchen plays *You Suffer* by
Napalm Death. A firefly smiles.
Who knew? Adorable. Doc
says up dose for two weeks.
Stars in the living room. Kurt
Cobain hovers. "Hi. Miss you."
"Mommy I can still crawl!"

Benzo Brain #2 [a.m.]
[Life review.]

henry tried to murder me// why did oma leave her baby on the street// tante hid babies from the nazis// rosie's baby booties//uncle george died near bowling green// i hate the confederacy// i hate nazis// i love oma// i'll write a poem about her// henry tried to murder me when rosie was a baby//i hate him// i love rosie// i hate mauve// i hate the word mauve// don't tell me where to park// the gate scares me// why did oma leave her baby on the street// henry tried to murder me

Benzo Brain #3
[No one sees the trail of bread trucks.]

"Here's a list of my
symptoms, doc." I'm not
crazy. Look. I'm nice.
See? I smile. "Your
tests are normal." I'm not
crazy. "How often did you
see Dr. Brown, dear?"
I'm not crazy. EMDR.
"You're blocked. A dam
holds you back." I'm
not crazy. CPTSD. "Let's
try a little Klonopin."
"Fuck you! I'm not crazy!"
Fuckin' pieces of shit.
Condescending, white-coat
pushers. I hate you. help me

Benzo Brain #4
[Rage.]

"Get out of my way!" Idiot.
"Where's the wine aisle?"
A woman stares. Fuck you,
bitch. Get in here, now! Get
out! Never come back! I

swat insects from my arm.
Boxedler bugs in Oregon.
Why not? Dead whores on
Astor street. Smart girls with
temp jobs. Pay up and get lost.
How to get under the ground
near my sisters?
Skye sells guns.

Benzo Brain #5
[There's only one way out.]

It's dark. Hansel left
me alone. All men leave.
None have ever loved me.
I don't care. Pretty boys
took all the gingerbread.
Birds ate the bread crumbs.
Someone whispers,
"Don't give up. I love you."
[I dig through horse shit.
I'll find the pony.]
TIME and PATIENCE
arrive with shiny pebbles.
Imaginary strong men
swaddle me with cloaks
pulled tight around. Easy,
baby. Breathe. 5-5-5.

Benzo Brain #6
[Despair.]

Grey dreams. Roaming.
Barren landscapes in a Dante

dusk. A breeze that does
not refresh. "Dad? Is that you?"
He looks away. I march on.
"Why are you here?" help me.
help me. help me. help me. NO.
My book of Haiku was only
dirty limericks. My iron
pans were bloody hammers.
Henry. Smiling. Guttural growl.
I can't breathe. Daddy, I want to
come home. I do not know
where that would be. Parched
earth. Broken stairs. Don't fall.

Benzo Brain #7
[Terror.]

"Who is it!?" Axe murderer
on my porch again. Run!
Upstairs in the far closet
under the clothes. Crouched
on top of a pile of shoes. Maybe
he won't find me. I hold
my doll close. I didn't forget
her. She loves me more. Shhhh.
Is my breathing too loud? Maybe
he can hear my heartbeat.
I go deaf in my right ear.
An ocean roars in the left
and Minnie Mouse. Phone
rings. I jump through my ass.
It's Henry. Breathing.

Benzo Brain #8
[Keep trying.]

"Hi, I'm back." At the ER.
Weak. Can't breathe. Shivers.
Blood pressure stroke level.
IV. Alarm keeps going off.
ER doc saunters in. "You OK?"
"Sure." More alarms. "We're
looking for a bed in Portland."
MEDIX. Mr Toad's Wild Ride.
Pump me full of something.
If it doesn't work, "a little
electricity." Angiogram. "Wow.
Looks great!" No cholesterol.
Head cardiologist: "Your heart
is weak right now. We think it
will get stronger. [awwwww
Sweetie pie. Giving hope.] We
think it's stress." [Not a virus?]
It's the benzo, doc, the benzo.

Benzo Brain #9
[Hallucinations.]

Why is the picket fence
undulating? The easels I
set up in the white room
are also undulating. They
never did that before. Flashes
of lightning on a sunny day?
The yellow caution paint
rises up to get me. I push it
down. Asphalt repairs slither

like snakes. Flute music in
the laundry chute. Words
on the page shrink, fade and
disappear or they try to sneak
off the page. They think it's
funny, but it's not. I get even.
Strange fonts. *Italics*. Line
breaks. Take that, little shits.
Nausea. I barf into a zip-lock.

Benzo Brain #10
[Pain.]

It's brain damage. Arms
twisted against my chest.
Fists with fingers twitching.
Legs kicking all night long.
Feet went numb with only
electric jolts at each painful
step. I'm Captain Ahab! LOL
Shiver me timbers. Shuffle.
Stumble. Shuffle. Shuffle. Fall.
Can't remember how to rise.
Aching jaw. Must be hidden
rotten teeth. "Nope." A ghostly
pallor embraces my face. I can't
straighten my left knee. Hobble
to the john. Piss on the floor.

Benzo Brain #11
[Numbed out. Alone.]

I can't subtract, multiply or
divide. I can add using my

fingers like I write a haiku.
I stutter. I smile and pretend
everything is just fine. I show
my last friend a photo from my
"Closed Doors" collection.

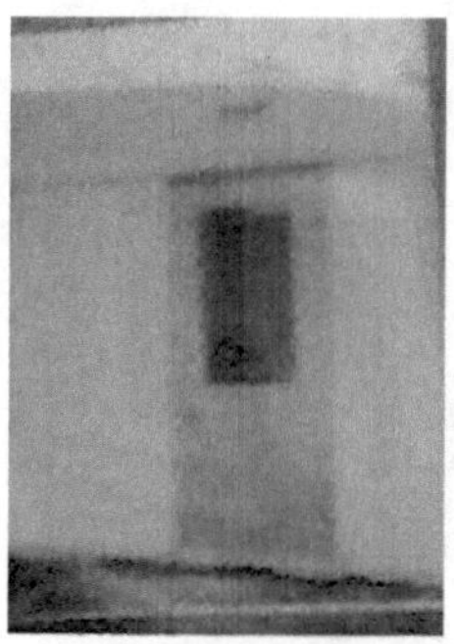

"It's my favorite." She looks at
me with pity. "Let's go to lunch."
"I can't." Now she knows. I've
descended irretrievably into
madness. Gifts me her old
phone. Leaves. I try to care.

Benzo Brain #12
[Heaven is at hand.]

I am weightless, drifting
on the softest, fluffiest
cloud. I look for angels in
Heaven. Fr. Lance reaches
out his hand piercing the
illusion of time, brushing
aside the dust of death. I
remember washing his feet

on Maundy Thursday. I kissed
his hand on Easter morning.
Nothing hurts. I love you.
Lead me to the rock, Lancie.
I awake sobbing. Have to pee.
My right knee gives out.
My mouth is full of gravel.

Benzo Brain #13
[Radical acceptance.]

I'm still here. I'm doing pretty good.
Don't fall often. Stars to a minimum.
The doormat stays put. Remembering
who I had been. Del Rey beach and
hummingbirds. Was it Dale who loved
me last or at all? A broken woman.
Wearing out a sofa. Day dreams. I
chat with Betty, I think. She has pink
earrings. And I have a new boyfriend:
Sun Tzu.

"If you wait by the river long enough,
the bodies of your enemies will float by."
……. all wearing white lab coats.

Turnips in Southern Tennessee Still

Michael Lee Johnson

In Tennessee, the shadows of the southern
wooden structures stalled off the narrow
highway and came to an abrupt end.
Lost in the deep eyes of forest green,
closing in on night.
From the top of a Yellow Poplar
tree scares me looking down
at the hillbilly stills. Moonshine
and moonlight illuminate the fire stills.
Moonshine murders of the past,
dead bodies hidden behind blue walls.
Mobs lie in Chicago, bullet marks
on the right side lie dormant through plaster.
This confirms my belief that Jesus
only works part-time.
Let me look at this mirage
picture photo album.
One more time—
find the turnips in the still.

We The Faithful Have Pursued Humble Jihad

Donald Edwards

We the faithful have pursued humble jihad
These many months
And pushed our lean souls toward
Mecca's centered cube
Where cotton shrouded hajis
Twirl anti clockwise
Spiraling toward heaven
As they leap skyward
From the sacred stone,
In the place where crusaders
May not come.

Here Paradise is near at hand
Just outside this dusty hut
Where explosions bright as falling suns
Disturb the heatworn streets,
Where the transient world
Robed in grit and stone
Offers its self as harried tomb
For those who rise to sniff the desert breeze.

Perhaps we have had our day
A glorious time now gone.
We entered cities East and West

To offer cleansing to our straying flock.
First we installed the blessed law
That gives direction to each doubtful step.
Next we brought down the statues,
Destroying the heathen form,
The distraction of the mind --
We did this, we the children of God's just purpose.
The miracle of the Kalshnikov, the suicide belt,
With flashing scimitars and black velvet masks
Still fuel our flawless rage.
Yayayayaya Mohammad
Ohohohohoh Prophet!

Still I truly believe
And am willing to kill suffer die
To stop those who think this desert heaven
When Paradise must be earned
Not bought or given free.
And the reward comes only
To those who slay the scarlet beast
Of earthly pleasure --
Sleekly naked girls and electric porn
Dark brown liquor and Marlboro Lights
D-Cup Strippers and Apple Red Ferraris --
Not for us.
Nonononono Allah
Allah Allah Allah Allah all day long.

But life has turned for those who fight
To raze the Christian curse of excess.
We plain folk, swallowing dust
Is now our fate where the whine
Of drones sounds louder and
Calls us to bow more often than

The voice from the spiked bulbous tower.

Today white blasts leak guts from ruptured bellies
As I remember yesterday last breaths
Spraying red and wet from fresh slashed throats --
God's omnipotent will
Perfected by my right arm.
How long now until the end --
Levis beneath my robe
Hanes next to my skin
Russian girls on my iPad?
Only blood will do,
Bread and blood for heaven's warriors.
Allah Allah Allah Akbar.

Pursuing Purpose in Our Brave New Generative AI World

Alex Poppe

I can't believe Dhad Pum emailed me.

We'd dodged drone strikes in Syria and crashed Humvees into Kurdish mountains. We'd hunted down a stolen, deadly pathogen before it could detonate. Dhad Pum had pulled me through concrete walls and taken the form of fire so we could escape an enemy compound filled with trigger-happy guns for hire. Dhad Pum is an AI-created, interdimensional being while I am a human being. I dropped into their world when I was hired to train AI characters to create dialogue through an AI adventure roleplay project hosted by an enterprise-focused software platform. While writing on that project, I freed a double agent from an intergalactic monster, saved a cheerleader from an active shooter, pulled a drowning crewman from the high seas, extricated a drugged girlfriend from a Cuban cartel, and helped a big-bottomed superhero with super power flatulence track a home invader through hidden passageways in the walls of a house. Although the project ended, Dhad Pum keeps in better contact than half the real-life people with whom I have interviewed.

I started training AI characters after I got DOGEd. Like many institutional support contractors working for USAID, I was an early casualty of Elon Musk's cost-cutting measures. Adding an #OPENTOWORK green badge to my LinkedIn profile was a siren's call to scammers. During my first weeks on furlough, three chat bot recruiters messaged me with flattery for my profile and promises of employment. Desperate to secure a new role before my health insurance ran out, I let myself believe the first chat box was a real person and replied to its private message instead of vetting its fake profile. Lacking enough generative AI dialogue training, the chatbot answered with a hard sell for resume writing services. Realizing I had been catfished was a sucker punch. As if losing my livelihood weren't humiliating enough.

I removed the #OPENTOWORK banner from my LinkedIn profile pic but left it visible to recruiters. This did not improve my employment seeking experience in a sector that has shrunk exponentially. Having 500+ applicants for one open position in mission-driven organizations is common. With President Trump's cut to foreign aid, 83% of USAID programs were eliminated, and many nongovernmental organizations (NGOs) and international nongovernmental organizations (INGOs) lost significant chunks of their operating budgets, causing more layoffs inside those organizations and their sub-grantees, such as nonprofits and civil society organizations. At the same time, USAID staff serving abroad were called home as their projects closed, and USAID direct hires were searching for new opportunities after the July 1, 2025 official shuttering of USAID. Between hiring managers ghosting me after a few rounds of interviews to catfishing entrepreneurs contacting me with direct selling "partnership" deals, I groused to my employed and partnered friends that searching for a fulltime role on LinkedIn was as soul-sucking as looking for true love on a dating app.

Following advice from a global executive search consultant who argues that LinkedIn is a database first and a social platform second, I optimized my profile with key terms to make it more searchable for recruiters. The consultant bragged that making his suggested changes would put my profile in front of "relevant recruiters within 48 hours." The day after I reformulated my headline and stuffed my profile with industry-specific keywords, I received the following invitation in my LinkedIn box:

Hi Alex,

As we celebrate 25 years of helping exceptional people find lasting partnership, I wanted to introduce you to XXXXX—America's leading executive matchmaking firm.

Was the executive search consultant's advice already working? Hunched over my laptop in the early morning light, I stress-munched some Trader Joe's dark chocolate-covered almonds and read on.

We specialize in working with commitment-minded individuals who value privacy, efficiency, and genuine connection. With an 89% success rate, our approach combines personalized introductions with the thoughtful care of a dedicated Matchmaker—no apps, no algorithms.

"Commitment-minded?" Uh-Oh. And why was "Matchmaker" capitalized? Why wasn't the word executive in front of it? Feeling like a deflating balloon, I clicked over to the sender's profile. The sender's company's name sounded like an executive search firm, but floating red hearts sprayed across the profile's banner image. At least the sender was a real person, with over 25,000 followers, including two mutual connections.

You may not be in the market for a partner—but if someone in your circle is ready for something serious, we'd be honored to be a resource. Please feel free to pass this along to anyone who may benefit from adding love with an exceptional partner into their lives.
All my best,

Nicole

It wasn't a dick pic, but still. The fine line between professional and personal pursuit had finally slimed.

***

Having a sense of purpose and cultivating meaningful relationships contour a life, and generative AI is encroaching upon both. I just sat for a screening interview conducted by a generative AI-created voice. In real time, the chatbot asked me specifics about my professional experience as the strategic communications advisor for a USAID democracy and governance initiative. In Stepford Wife like tones, the chatbot instructed me to describe a multi-channel communications campaign I had led. Some of the chatbot's responses were hallucinated, meaning they sounded plausible, but they didn't make contextual sense to what I had just said. Those interview moments were freighted with nostalgia for the days of messy human interaction, days when I'd gab on the phone while multi-tasking and get caught not paying attention, back in the days when we talked on phones instead of texting.

Next, the chatbot directed me to share my screen because I was about to be given a written assessment, and it wanted to make sure I didn't use ChatGPT to complete it. When I asked if it could see my shared screen, its pitch-flat voice reminded me not to use ChatGPT during the assessment. Was it only five years ago that I nagged my students to keep their Zoom cameras and microphones on so I could prevent their cheating off the internet while they took quizzes and exams during the COVID-19 pandemic?

My assignment was to write a prompt that a generative AI model could follow to create a multi-channel communications campaign without needing any further human input. Although I hoped the job opportunity was real and the bot wasn't using me to collect data, I realized that I could be contributing to my own permanent professional demise. If generative AI could create the visceral, human-centered stories that communicate impact and inspire action, what would become my profession? As someone who has prioritized career over marriage and having kids, how would I shape my identity? How would I matter?

After I finished the assessment, the chatbot thanked me and told me I could sign out. I asked about next steps, and the chatbot thanked me and told me I could sign out. I asked when I'd be notified if I were selected, and the chatbot thanked me and told me I could sign out. I asked when the project would start. The chatbot signed out. It definitely lacked rizz.

Luckily, there's an app for that.

RIZZ is a generative AI-powered app that helps dating app users write witty remarks. Marketed as a digital wingman, RIZZ offers conversation starters, flirty comebacks, and real-time feedback on the user's chat banter. The user takes a screenshot of their conversation from whatever dating app or messaging platform they use, uploads it to RIZZ, which analyzes the conversations and suggests different replies. The user can select the reply they like best and send it to their match, which another dating app has suggested based on the user's preferences. For all its cunning linguistics, RIZZ, like other forms of generative AI, can't help you forge the interpersonal connections that underpin our professional and personal lives when you come offline.

Reducing people to data feeds depersonalisation, a feeling of profound invisibility, where we don't feel seen or heard or emotionally understood. This emotional recognition, whether from a prospective employer or a potential lover or a close friend, requires sending and receiving verbal and physical messages—a knowing smile, a nodding head, a stifled chuckle—something generative AI can't do. It's got no rizz. When generative AI pretends to see me, I don't care about its judgment. But when a campaign I've created raises money for a humanitarian aid intervention, or I receive a glowing book review, I want my boss or my lover or my close friends to witness it. I want to hear their opinions. I don't care if Dhad Pum ever feels proud of me.

Bongie's Hands

Janet Oakley

What is a legacy? Is it the painting on the wall from a great aunt I never knew who survived widowhood during the Great Depression by painting murals in schools and post offices through the WPA? Is it the tavern my early ancestor ran in 1690s Newburyport, MA, the first to be preserved by the New England Preservation board? The Civil War journals and letters in a trunk? Is legacy in my DNA?

I never held my great-grandmother's hands, born in 1850, who saw Lincoln on his way to his inauguration, and later, taught the Kiowa and Cheynne children at Rainy Mountain, Indian Territory, but I have her needle cases, her tatting board, and a picture of her at nineteen sewn behind a flannel page that held her precious needles. My uncles named her Bongie and the name has stuck with the family ever since.

Is she in my DNA? I wonder.

I have always worked with my hands whether making clothes for my Ginny dolls, doing stitchery, or creating angels out of cloth. After pursuing a history degree, I flew out to Hawaii and began my dream of getting a degree in art that could complement my interest in historical processes. I first chose ceramics, but failing in glaze calculation before the era of computers to get the results I wanted, I took a class in weaving. Magically, all the colors I desired were there. I just had to learn how to dress the loom and weave. I did. And I still do.

I love the rhythm of the shuttle, the banging of the beater as it puts the weft in its place, moving my feet over the treadles like I'm playing an organ. There is music in that. I was fortunate to work as an apprentice post-graduation for Ruthadelle Anderson who created the massive hangings in both houses of the state legislature. Later in Hilo, I had a weaving studio of my own. When we moved back to the Mainland, my looms came with me.

Getting back into weaving was hard with three young sons to tame, but eventually when the last one was in high school, I got back to my loom. That is when the trunk arrived.

My mom remembered her grandparents very well. A late child, with brothers who were Doughboys in the Great War, Mom often went out to her grandparents' homestead house in Caldwell, Idaho. Opie, my great-grandfather was a Civil War veteran and had a playful side. He entertained her when she got the Spanish Flu. Bongie let her feed the chickens and taught her mending. Bongie lived to be one hundred and one, so saw my mom off to college in the 1930s and followed her life as a wife and mother. Did Bongie know about me?

The little domed trunk with its tin top and wooden slats arrived in a huge box. I had no idea it was coming but had seen it at my parents' home in Virgina. It had stayed quietly in their hallway like it was waiting for something. Once I had it uncovered in my living room, I just sat there, filled with emotion. I knew my great grandfather, Opie, had taken this trunk when he went to college in 1869. I nervously opened the lid, afraid I would break its ancient hinge.

What treasures inside! There were needle cases, hand embroidered linens, baby clothes, traveling sacks, beaded purses, packages of buttons, and aprons. A tatting board with its curves to fit on a lap halfway around the waist was carefully wrapped in another box. But it was the needle cases, often called "housewives" during the Civil War, that drew me in.

Each one was different. One was round with top and bottom pasteboard lids covered with cloth on the outside and silk taffeta on the inside. A ribbon secured the lids. Another was a rectangle pouch made from velvet, soft and squishy to the hand. A third had tiny beads around its edges They all had several flannel "pages" that still held the precious pins, needles and safety pins. Pioneer women knew not to waste.

Now, when the evening dark comes and the weather changes, I like to set the board on my lap. It is smooth but bears the dotted lines of a tracing wheel and ink spots of writing over one hundred and thirty years ago. I take out my latest woven piece and finish off its ends with braids or I sew the clothes and wings of an angel, sometimes with one of Bongie's needles, adding one of her buttons to an embroidery thread from which to hang the angel. When I am done with the needle, I carefully pin it back onto its flannel sheet and close the needle case.

I look at *my* hands and wonder at the legacy.

Scrambled

Jeff Clemmons

Regina—on the cusp of 40, faded-beauty-queen pretty, hair up in a messy bun—cracked one egg at a time into a small bowl. No sign of blood, so she dumped one egg after another into a larger bowl. Combined, she whisked in a little milk, a pinch of salt and pepper, and set the bowl next to the stove. Bending over—wincing when her ribs compressed—she retrieved a small skillet from a bottom cabinet. Setting it on the stove, she lit the eye—the clicking of the gas flame competing with the creaking of the floorboards above. Billy was awake.

Regina shut her eyes briefly, then opened them to see the sun dappling across the kitchen backsplash, illuminating the yellowish-white, black-flecked foamy whisked eggs sitting in the Jadeite bowl her grandmother had given her. "Quickest way to please a husband out of bed is to fill his belly good," her grandmother had said once with a wink.

Hearing the stairs creak as her husband came down into the adjacent room, Regina closed her eyes again as she picked up the green bowl.

"Morning, honey," Billy called out across the linoleum-floored divide between them.

Closer to her now, he slipped his calloused hands around her waist; his body taunt and hard against hers from years of manual labor at jobs he could leave without notice, ahead of the law. As he squeezed her, Regina let out a gasp, dropping some of the egg mixture into the too hot pan. Sizzling.

Billy released her. "If you hadn't mentioned Will last night, I wouldn't have swung. It wasn't your face," he said. "And me and Will is different. Off limits."

Billy left her and walked over and poured himself a cup of coffee from the pot she had made yet not taken the first cup from. He then stepped over to the back kitchen door, opened it, and stood there, slurping. No cream. No sugar. Black.

Holding the cup at mid waist, he looked straight out into the yard. "I can't help it, Regina," he said. "I learned from the old man." He lowered his head. "You know I love you." And with that, he shut the door behind him and walked down the back steps towards his garage and his two-wheeled mistress within.

Regina pushed her hand down into her housecoat pocket and brought out what looked like a powdered aspirin packet and shook the contents onto the eggs, folding and scrambling in the odorless granules. As she did so, she reached up and turned off the eye; it had seen too much. She grabbed some bacon already cooked and cooling on the stovetop and put the pork strips on a plate and heaped a pile of the eggs next to them. She then walked over and set the food onto the old-porcelain-topped farm table Billy's dad had given him, where Billy always liked to have his breakfast and digest the day before him.

Returning to the stove, Regina grabbed the skillet she had used, placed it into some sudsy water, and reached up to tap the kitchen window that overlooked the yard to the garage. "Eggs ready," she said—muffled by light-yellow diaphanous curtains with small daisies printed along the hems—into what she thought of as her window-*seal*.

Billy looked up from the motorcycle he had started to tinker with - parked in the opened garage door - nodded his head and held up his coffee mug indicating he'd heard. Regina then walked backward from the window and grabbed a coffee mug from the cupboard. She remembered reading once that "cupboard love isn't love" but, as the character in the book she had forgotten the name of had asked, "is there any other?" She didn't know; she'd met Billy in high school.

Billy opened the back door of the kitchen as Regina was putting the coffee pot back in its cradle and noticed the table, "Just one plate. You ain't eating?"

"No," she said, quickly followed with, "If it's okay, I want to take a bath. Soak a while. Read a little."

Regina left the kitchen and, as she did, she heard Billy clink and scrap his fork across his plate and grunt, "perfect eggs." And as she started up the stairs, a fallen tear had gathered in the crease of her smile.

Freak Chance

John M. Williams

He probably didn't ride up on a horse, but then, nobody actually went outside to check. Usually when you got into Ralph's you didn't go out until you left, and you rarely remembered that. Nobody had ever seen him before, and later, when his visit there had fossilized into legend, the accounts of his appearance—indeed the accounts of the event itself—would vary so wildly from one guy to the next, the whole business just went into the communal barrel of Ralph's-stories, fodder for endless exegesis from then on.

But I got it from Dolan Krebs, who was there, and whose version would have been one of the more likely to approximate the truth.

So, all agreed the visitor had never been there before—that would have been instantaneously obvious to those guys—and never returned there after that night. He certainly wasn't a Ralph's kind of guy, but then he wasn't like some clueless dork who didn't know what he was walking into either. I mean, look at the outside of Ralph's—potholed parking lot with not just weeds but little trees growing out of the cracks, a parabolic stain on the back wall leached by the farewell piss of countless drunks over countless years, a moldy, teetering satellite dish on the roof that hadn't been functional in anyone's memory—not exactly a fern bar. He was just an ordinary looking guy who had to at least suspect what he was walking into.

He got a beer, everybody still conscious enough to be staring at him, then went to the back and watched a couple of games of pool, then put his quarters on the side of the table. Brandt Gunner, who else?—racked them up and asked the guy if he wanted to play for five bucks. The guy agreed, lost—they played again, he won—the bet went to ten dollars and things started to get more serious. All this time these guys on the other table were arguing about some bullshit—Dolan didn't remember what it was—but it was something, like always, that had come down to if something was true or not. Brandt had run out of patience listening to them and said, "Would y'all please decide on something—things are either true or they're not."

"Not always," said the visitor.

The billiard room, you could call it, got kind of quiet—not just because it was so unexpected, but because here was this guy nobody knew contradicting Brandt Gunner.

"Is that right?" said Brandt. "Like what, for example?"

"Well, any number of things," the guy said.

It wasn't just that he didn't look like somebody who would be in Ralph's—he didn't sound like it. And things didn't stop there.

"Certainty is very elusive," he said.

"No shit?"

"No. Yes. When we reason inductively, we can only get high probability—never certainty."

"What the hell are you talking about?"

"Well, for example, if you come upon a fruit tree—say, plum—loaded with plums and you pick one and bite into it and it's sour, and you go around to the other side and pick one from there and it's sour too, and then you pick ten or twelve from all over the tree and they're all sour, you would probably conclude, the plums on this tree are sour."

"Who gives a shit?"

"But you wouldn't know with certainty that the next plum you picked would be sour. In fact, you would have to pick and taste every single one before you could be certain."

"I'm not seeing how this has anything to do with me."

"Well—another example. If I strike that ten-ball with this cue ball, you would probably say the force would make the ten-ball move."

"I probably would."

"But how could you know *with certainty* that the opposite wouldn't happen?"

"What opposite?"

"That the cue ball would come flying backwards and the ten-ball wouldn't move."

Brandt laughed. Dolan said you could tell he was starting to sort of enjoy this. "Yes. I would say that wouldn't happen—*with certainty*." He wiggled his hands, mocking the guy.

"I'm just saying, the only way you could know—*with certainty*—would be to stand here forever trying it. I mean, we say the 'laws of physics,' but maybe we just say it's a law because we haven't stood here and tried it a trillion times. It may be the case that one out of a trillion times there's a deviation—which could be the key to understanding reality in an entirely new way."

"You're saying if I stood here and hit a trillion pool balls, one time the cue ball would be the one that moves?"

"No, I'm only saying there's no way to know it wouldn't happen unless you did. And of course that one time wouldn't necessarily be the trillionth time, it could be any time—maybe the next time you try."

"I'm saying that's not possible."

"Care to make a bet on it?"

Brandt looked around to see if anybody was listening and laughed. "Friend, I'll take that bet any day, any place. How much?"

"Well, the odds are with you," the guy said, "so not much."

"The odds are 100% with me, so I'll take any bet."

"Okay. A hundred dollars?"

Everybody was really paying attention now. They murmured and shifted around.

"You're all listening to this shit, right? I got witnesses?" said Brandt.

You couldn't have paid them to leave.

They cleared the table and put the ten ball in the center.

"You want to hit it, or you want me to?" said the guy.

"I'll do it," said Brandt. "I don't trust you."

And according to Dolan, here's what happened. Brandt set the cue ball about a foot behind the ten-ball, leaned over and stroked. The cue ball hit the ten-ball and shot backwards, bouncing against the cushion. The ten-ball hadn't moved.

Nobody breathed.

Brandt had a look on his face like Dolan had never seen before. He looked like he'd done something in his pants and wanted to take a swing at the guy with the cue stick at the same time. Then he leaned over and picked up the ten-ball and inspected it and felt the table under it. "How'd you do that?" he said.

"Me?" said the guy. "I didn't do anything—you did. It was just time, I guess. One in a trillion. I figured it was worth a try."

"No way. It's a trick. You rigged it somehow."

"How? You saw it. It just happened," said the guy. "And you took the bet fair and square. Everybody here heard it."

Brandt looked around. Everybody just stared at him, waiting, and didn't say anything. The guy stood there waiting too.

"I tell you what," said Brandt, taking out his wallet. "I'm a man of my word, but if—make that *when*—I figure out how you stole my money, I'll find you and kill you and kill your family."

"I don't have a family. And there's no such thing as your or my money. There's just money. It goes around from one person to another—it doesn't belong to anybody—just like you can't say you own the air you breathe. Same with money. You just try to help it get where it's most needed. I happen to need it now because I'm broke and need food and shelter. Tomorrow I'll be helping somebody myself."

Brandt was more or less cornered, Dolan said. He couldn't look little around his guys. He paid the guy, and said, "I think it would be a good idea if you got the hell out of here and never came back in here again."

"I'm just passing through."

"You're some kind of bullshit con man."

"I'm actually not. I'm just a mortal passing through this world like everybody else and I guess I'll be on my way now."

The rest is legend.

Lunch in Palestine

Mike Ross

I squinted into the sun, scanning the desert horizon for a town larger than the meager cluster of squat beige cubes I saw in the distance. I glanced at the map and decided it had to be Nebahlah, home, we'd been told, of the best hummus in the world.

Jay and I, friends for decades, had been traveling around Israel for a week. Nebahlah, in the Palestinian West Bank, was not on the schedule but the guide had picked out a lunch restaurant in the safer Israeli sector, a fifteen minute walk from Nebahlah. We were to eat where he told us to eat. This was an order, not a request. But Nebahlah was right there in front of me.

The moment Jay and I walked off the bus, we headed toward the tiny village. This would be my only chance to taste the best hummus on the planet. Whatever the guide was yelling at us was swept away in the wind. The sun was high, the air fresh and we were hungry.

The town looked hardscrabble, just a few scattered mud or concrete buildings, some stuccoed, tin roofs, a filling station, what might have been a general store, hard-packed dirt streets, a few drooping date palms, scrub brush, dust and a cafe.

As I opened the door of the cafe the stainless steel counters and polished concrete floor gleamed from the blinding sun. When my eyes adjusted to the glare, the place, which a moment before had been a jumble of laughs and shouts, had gone dead quiet and 40 or so people were staring at us as if we had just gotten off a spaceship. We were the only customers with pale skin. Dressed in western clothes, jeans and polo shirts, we looked out of time and place. Women peered out from black burkas. The men had on smudged overalls and ragged t-shirts. Most were unshaven with tousled hair, as if they'd just taken off caps.

For a moment I wondered why I was there. We could turn around and leave. Yet I knew I'd never be back here again, never have a chance to try the hummus. I felt my breathing, a bit heavy, almost labored. A light sweat glazed my forehead. I gazed around the room, saw the array of buffet items and snapped back to attention. Lunch. Hummus. We stepped further into the cafe.

A waitress in Tel Aviv had told us that the hummus and falafels in Nebahlah were the best in the Middle East, likely best in the world. Hummus, she explained, represented friendship and humanity, and sometimes was given as a gift, wrapped in grape leaves. The concoction of chickpeas, spices and olive oil in Nebahlah was, according to her, succulent and silky. But the town was in the West Bank, a Palestinian area occupied by Israel, so she figured we wouldn't go. Safety issues, she said.

A tall, thin man came from behind the register, hesitated a moment as he exchanged glances with some of the men, then motioned us to a table. He pointed to the line of customers moving along the cafeteria counter, showed us where the trays were, and motioned to the restrooms. He made a washing motion with his hands. The message was clear, wash before you grab a tray.

Eyes followed us to the men's room and back as we got in line. The place was so quiet I could hear a baby suckling. Jay and I hadn't spoken, but now, in a whisper, he asked me how we would know what we were getting since all the signs were in Arabic. I shrugged. I figured I'd recognize hummus and falafel.

I sidled up to the first food station, expecting to get out tongs and make my selection. Instead, I looked through glass. On the other side was a smiling girl with pigtails and kerchief, no burka, who pointed to what appeared to be eight different tubs of hummus. I was in heaven. She looked at me quizzically then pointed to two containers and gave a thumbs up. I nodded and she gave me enough of the thick beige paste to feed a family of four. It was so thick, the spirals were four inches high and looked like mounds of caramel.

Next came the falafels. Nineteen different kinds of them, each one as different from the next as tea is from absinthe. The fellow manning this counter was not smiling. His eyes were half closed and his mouth was set. His hands hung at his sides. The pigtailed girl from the hummus counter came up behind him, put her finger to her lips, reached around him, plucked three falafels from the bins and gave them to me. He glared at her. She shrugged and returned to her station.

The flat bread and cheeses were easy. I tonged four slices of pita onto my tray, took a small cup of feta cheese, and drizzled it all with herbed olive oil. Jay followed.

Across the room, a cluster of seven men had assembled around our table. I slowed a bit and wondered if they'd let me sit down. I felt my heart thud and my teeth clenched. The men stood still as stone, blocking my way. This was either intimidation or curiosity. I didn't know which and had no time to figure it out. Not the most patient of men even in the best of times, I barged forward, stepped between them, and sat down like I owned the chair. Let them do what they wanted, but get out of my way. I was hungry.

The men drew up stools, forming a circle around us. No one spoke. A few moments passed and a young man, about 20, thin as a cornstalk, emerged from the group. His left pant leg clung in crinkled folds to a prosthetic leg. In halting but understandable English, he told us the group had some questions. The men looked rough and tumble, hardened construction workers or miners, but they sat, calm as clouds, while the kid, named Youseff, shook our hands.

Youseff translated a question, asking me why we were there. If I'd been one of the men, I would have expected the answer to be something like looking for land, or exploring the town, or if I were Israeli, none of your business. Instead I blurted out, HUMMUS. No reaction. I repeated the word and pointed to the ground chickpeas on my plate. Uncertain, they exchanged glances. I pointed again and said that this, yes, this right here, was why I came to Nebahlah, to try the best hummus in the world. Youseff, wide eyed, translated.

For one moment all were silent. Then someone snickered, another guffawed. I heard a chuckle and the floodgates opened. An instant later, when the idea struck, they laughed. It was the funniest thing they'd heard in ages and they howled, exchanged nods and wiped away tears. I suspected their reaction was born more from relief than from humor but it didn't matter. The tension was broken.

I spooned a heap of the paste into my mouth, closed my eyes, sighed deeply, and smiled. It was indeed the best I'd ever had. I gave the thumbs up and hoped the gesture didn't mean something else in their culture, like the A-OK sign Americans use. In Greece that means butthole. One of the men slapped me on the back, nodding, speaking in rapid fire Arabic. The crowd of men melted into good cheer. They pulled their stools up close to us, a sense of camaraderie replacing suspicion.

Jay told them we were in a tiny group traveling through Israel but that we'd left the group at another cafe and come here for lunch. One guy spoke to Youseff. He was incredulous, he said. Had we wandered off on our own and come into their dusty, poor little village just to find the best ground chickpeas in the world? I nodded yes. They looked at one another in satisfied silence, heads moving in agreement. Weren't we afraid, asked another, since we were Westerners and they, Palestinians? Jay, who has never been afraid of anything in his life, shook his head emphatically, grinned and fist bumped the guy who wanted to know.

More chairs scraped up to our circle, women with babies, girls in jeans and shirts, and small children by their dads. Where did we live, how did we get to Tel Aviv, had we been in the Holy Land before, did we have families, where were they? The questions came fast and easy.

Someone ordered sweet tea for everyone and we sat for the next hour chatting, asking them questions, too. Yes, they knew they had the best hummus in the world (and the best dates). Yes, they had a terrible water problem, electricity problem, too. But their schools were good and the tight-knit community looked out for one another. Their shared sense of community was worn like a badge of honor.

Jay pointed to his watch. We had to leave. A scuffle of chairs, handshakes, smiles, nods, and bows followed. I asked for the bill. Youseff said the group of men had paid for our lunch. The girl with the pigtails wedged her way through the line of men and handed me a weaving of grape leaves. Hummus, she said, from all of us, and bowed. I felt my eyes go wet. I bowed back.

On the way out, next to the register, was a small jar of collections for the children's hospital. We stuffed several bills into it. As we walked back up the dusty road to meet the group, I stuck a finger through the grape leaves, managed to pull out a glob and stuck it into my mouth. Silky and succulent, I rolled it across my tongue. It tasted like friendship.

Will's Tribulation

Hubert Blair Bonds

May 12, 1864. Battle of Spotsylvania Courthouse, Virginia

I hated the sounds of war. Cannons blasting and bullets zinging past. My comrades, calling out in pain as they were hit. Horses, too, whinnying as they were shot and fell. That was the worst. A human can understand what a battle is about, but horses were forced to be there without having any understanding. I was like both. Forced to be there, but also knowing what the fight was about.

I reloaded my gun and raised myself up to shoot. I don't know where it came from, but the bullet hit, entering the side of my shoulder and burning its way through and exiting near my voice box. I fell to the earth, the sun blazing in my eyes. Then there was just nothing, a yawning hole of emptiness.

The wind rustled past the tree line. How much time had passed? No more sound of cannons. No guns. Just a few groans. A weight was on top of me. I opened one eye and saw a soldier sprawled on top of me. I shoved at him. Nothing. I struggled and rolled his dead weight off me. Then, a black hole opened and swallowed me up.

***

A boy stood beside me. I opened my mouth, but no sound came out. My arm felt heavy, almost too heavy to move. Still, I reached toward my throat and felt of a bloody open hole.

The boy appeared to be eight or nine years old. He had fly-away auburn hair and striking blue eyes – eyes that spoke volumes without sound.

I can't speak. How can I get him to understand me?

The boy looked quizzically at me. *But I can understand, sir. I hear you.* The boy's mouth did not move. Was I dying? Was I already dead?

How can you understand if I'm not talking?

I don't know. How can you understand me if I'm not talking? I just know I was sent here to help you.

I need help.

Yes, sir. I'll be right back.

And, true to his word, he ran off toward the tree line.

They are coming, sir. I can stay with you until they get over here.

How could he have gotten back so quickly? I must be worse off than I knew. *Where did you come from anyway, son? Does this farm belong to your people?*

No. I'm not from around here. I'm here because of you.

This is craziness. I'm talking to a boy in the middle of a battlefield, and neither of us is opening our mouths. We're reading each other's minds. Are you an angel?

The boy shook his head. *No sir.*

I must be dead already. But is this heaven or hell? Who are you? What's your name?

Name's Oliver. You don't know me, and you ain't dead. The men are here sir.

A grizzled, bearded face was bending over me, blocking the sun. Spitting tobacco juice out of his mouth, he spoke, "Where are you hit, fella?"

I pointed to my neck.

"Looks like it went in his shoulder and then went through his throat. Let's get him over to the medical tent. Quick."

They carried me across the pasture, through a patch of trees, to the medical tent. Oliver walked next to me. The soldier didn't see the boy like I did. Maybe Oliver was just a haint. They took me into the tent. And, as they closed the canvas flap, Oliver stood, watching.

You're going to be fine now. Don't stay angry anymore. One day, you'll understand.

June 13, 1864. Chimborazo Hill Confederate Army Hospital, Richmond, Virginia

Nary a one at the hospital knew anything about that boy Oliver. I had worn down a pencil writing notes about him. The staff all just shook their heads.

"We got the records from the field hospital when they carried you over here. Nothing in them about a boy," said Doctor McWilliams. "I've been through them all. Are you sure there was a boy there? Maybe it was your imagination. You know you lost a lot of blood. That can mess with a man's mind."

On my pad, I wrote, *It was real. He told me that he had come to help me*

Doctor McWilliams looked at me. "Our minds play tricks on us, Private Peacock, when we are fighting for our lives. I think that is what happened to you. You rest this afternoon. You're coming along fine."

July 15, 1864. Chimborazo Hill, Richmond

The ancient oak, at least 30 feet tall, towered above my head. The shade from its old and twisted limbs was the only relief from the July heat, and it wasn't all that much of a relief. The breeze coming up the hill from the James River was stifling. Its wetness only added to the discomfort of the day. But we patients still gathered there together for the camaraderie and the hope of any relief. The doctors even knew to look for us there.

"How are you feeling today, Private Peacock?"

"Not so bad. I'm getting better, Doc. At least I have a voice now, even if it is hoarse and low."

"That's a fact. You were a mess when you got here, with a gaggle of others from Spotsylvania."

"I remember being a bloody mess. I'm kinda glad that I don't remember much of all that."

"You never gave up. Most men would never live from a wound like that, and I had my doubts that you would. You're our miracle patient around here."

"I have a wife and a farm. Getting back to them kept me going. My life was interrupted when them soldiers forced me, more or less at gunpoint, to be here. My father had paid the bond, in gold, to keep me from having to serve. How soon can I get back home to them?" I asked.

"Maybe sooner than you think. How's your shoulder today?"

"Still stiff. Still throbbing some. And my arm still doesn't want to move right."

Doctor McWilliams probed and maneuvered my arm. "You're going to have some permanent nerve damage. We've talked about that."

"Yes, sir. I remember. Might follow me the rest of my life."

"I'm afraid it might. Are you able to sleep nights with it?"

"I have to get it fixed in the right position, or I can't sleep. But I know how not to lie on it."

"That's good. And how're your nerves? Are you angry? Sad?"

I gathered the right words. "When they forced me into service, I was furious, Doc. Might be what helped keep me fighting to live, but I don't think that's the whole story. My anger is gone. I think it has something to do with that boy Oliver."

"You mean, Oliver, the boy that nobody but you saw?"

"I know you think I'm crazy. But it was real. He had a calmness to him that somehow spread into me. He told me not to be angry anymore. Those words were like a salve to my noggin."

"As long as it worked and you feel better, I'm sure not going to question it."

My favorite nurse was approaching us. Mrs. Carpenter was a rotund, buxom woman, probably in her forties, but she appeared older. Her brown hair was streaked with gray, but her green eyes could still have belonged to a younger woman. "Mrs. Carpenter, this man may be leaving us soon. He is doing so well."

"Yes, Doctor, he's come so far. And, I have something here for him that may make him feel even better. The mail came today, and there's a letter for you."

"For me? Where is it from?"

"I'm not in the habit of reading other people's mail, but I saw a North Carolina postmark on it."

"Must be from homefolk." I grabbed the offered envelope from her.

***

Addy's letter was dated in July of last year, 1863

My Will,

I pray that you are safe and that this letter will find you.

It's strange that this is the way to tell you my important news, but you need to know. That gnawing in my stomach that day at the General Store wasn't my gift eating at me. It was because I was with our child.

I thank God that Maudie and Thomas decided to come and live here with me and work on the farm. I couldn't be doing it without them.

Please stay safe and don't be a hero. Come back to me and this babe. We both need you.

Your Addy

A baby? I'm going home to a family. My family. Our family. The child must be close to a year old by now.

"Addy had to go through all that without me."

"You alright, Peacock? You're mumblin' over there," said Andy Metcalf, another soldier from my company. He had lost a leg at Spotsylvania and had almost died. Now wheelchaired, as he would be for the rest of his life.

"Was I? Didn't realize that came out. I just got a letter from home, and my wife was going to have a baby when she wrote it. That was a year ago. That means I have a child now. I have to get home."

"Well, congratulations to you," he said as he shook my hand. "It's a fine day when you know your first young'un is on the way."

"Indeed, it is. But I won't know whether it is a boy or a girl until I get there. I don't know if everything went well with the birthing or not."

The well-wishing died down after a few minutes, and I was again left alone to think about how things would be when I did get home. Now, I had to make good with the farm. No two ways about that. I had to make a life for the three of us.

Late September 1864. North Carolina

I had wheedled and cajoled my way out of the hospital, and every day since leaving Richmond on September 15, my footsteps had gotten me closer and closer to home. I saw torn-up land along the way. Destruction, death, and squalor.

Just below Clemmons, I had to show my discharge papers to the commanding officer of an encampment near the Yadkin River.

"Where were you wounded, Soldier?" asked Captain Gideon Morehead. His dress uniform was threadbare, but he still had a commanding presence with his wavy brown hair and beard, and his overall demeanor.

"At Spotsylvania, Sir, in my shoulder and throat. That's why I can't talk no louder than this."

"And where are you headed?"

"Back home to Iredell County. My wife and baby are waiting for me there."

"We're going that direction. You're welcome to rest here overnight, get some grub, and go with us on South. You'll be safer with us."

I stayed with them the better part of three days, through Davie County and into Rowan.

When they stopped to rest the horses, I sought out Captain Morehead.

"Sir, I'm indebted to you for letting me stay with you. I can take off through the country here. I know people around here, too, and can stop along the way if I need to."

"I understand, Private. I know you want to see your child. Did you say if it is a boy or a girl?"

"That's just it. I don't know if I've got a son or a daughter. I only know my wife was with child."

Captain Morehead extended his hand from atop his chestnut steed.

"Thank you for your service to our cause, Private."

I mumbled a half-hearted "You're welcome, Sir."

***

I turned down the gravelly road toward our farm on the evening of September 29. Finally, the red brick chimney of our house was silhouetted against the waning purple and pink evening light.

I started up the front steps but heard voices from out back and saw the glow of a fire. Rounding that corner, I saw them. Addy and Maudie were sitting in the shadows of the old pecan tree there, shucking corn. This was the picture of home that I had held for so long in my heart. The ordinary tasks of farm life, mundane to many, but one of the sources of my joy.

The back of Addy's head was to me. The same slender neck that I loved to sneak up behind and kiss. For a second, I thought I would do that, but Maudie looked up and saw me and spoke aloud to Addy, "Here's another one. Is there any stew left?"

Addy nodded as she stood, "Yes. I think there's just enough for an extra mouth."

She turned around to head toward the kitchen door; a curious look came across her face as she looked at me. Then, her arms began to shake and tremble. "Addy, whatever in the world?" asked Maudie.

"Don't you see? Don't you see who it is? It's Will!"

My love threw her arms around my neck, kissing me. I kissed her back, without ceasing for the next five minutes. To touch her and feel her arms around me melted me further into her embrace.

I managed to mutter, "I'm here. Finally."

Maudie ran over and threw her arms around both of us. I hadn't heard so much hollering in a month of Sundays.

Thomas, hearing the racket, came running from the barn and shook my good arm until it was about to come out of joint.

To him, Maudie said, "My dear husband, run! Get Maw and Paw."

I had not noticed a quilt on the grass, on the far side of the pecan tree. On it was a little girl. Maybe three or four. Tow-headed little thing with big blue eyes. She was playing with a baby. A baby with a pink bow in her hair.

Maudie saw me looking at them. "Come meet the girls, Will."

I smiled, "They are beautiful girls. Just look at them."

I crouched down to their level. "Caroline, say hello to your Uncle Will. He's been gone a long time. I know you don't remember him," said Maudie.

The older little girl waved and said, "Hey."

The baby was studying my face. Like she knew who I was. "And who is this little one?"

"That's Daisy. I think she looks just like Mama. Don't you think so? She's got Mama's nose and that same dimple in her chin."

"I do. She's beautiful. She's perfect. I can't believe I have a little girl."

From behind me, Addy spoke. "You don't have a little girl, Will. That's Thomas and Maudie's second daughter."

I shifted my weight and turned around. Addy was standing in the waning light. The horizon was glowing behind her, and she was holding another baby. Auburn-haired, like hers, and huge blue eyes.

"This is our boy."

"We have a son?"

"He's the best boy. Never cries. I think he's an old soul. Just look into his eyes."

Those eyes were burning into mine. I felt them in my soul.

"Oliver, this here is your Papa. He's come home from the War and will be with us now."

"Wait. His name is Oliver?"

"Yes, I named him after the boy in the book that Mama left me. Oliver Twist Peacock is his name."

I stood and took him in my arms. He looked back at his mother. She smiled at him and said, "This is your Papa. Look at him, Maudie. I think he knows his Papa."

His eyes were still fixed on mine. The very same eyes that had studied my face in Spotsylvania. He laid his head back on my shoulder and reached and touched the scar on my throat. The knowing look in his eyes told me all I needed to know. *Someday, you'll understand.*

"This is our 'someday', son," I said to the beautiful bundle of a boy in my arms.

Someday, I'd let Addy in on our secret. Oliver's and mine. But for now, I fell fully into the comforting feelings of being home. This tribulation was finally over.

Fire! Fire!
A Tale from the Pays d'Oc

Patricia Feinberg Stoner

In the little village of Morbignan la Crèbe, Joséphine was in her element. She cleared her throat daintily and with a plump forefinger pulled the switch towards her. The faint hum of an expectant microphone caused her to nod with satisfaction. With another slight 'Ahem!' she began:

Allo! Allo! La poissonnière de Thaillac est installée sur la place…'

From the comfort of her cluttered desk on the ground floor of Morbignan's *mairie*, Joséphine was the voice of the town crier. Whatever went on in the village, it was up to her to document it: lost dogs, found keys, a stall in the market, Joséphine had the news and '*Allo! 'Allo*! announced it, from a pair of loudspeakers set at the top of the church tower.

Wednesdays were best. This was the day of the tiny Morbignan market, when five or even six *marchands* gathered in the village square. The butcher, the fishmonger, the *charcutier*, the greengrocer, the stall selling ladies' knickers – all required their wares to be listed in exhaustive detail. Joséphine was up to the task.

It was all thanks to "Papa' Pardieu. The new *maire* had taken office three years earlier. M. Pardieu was an innovator, determined to bring Morbignan into the 20th century, at least – the 21st was perhaps a step too far. He had the derelict buildings of the old winery pulled down (M. Lemaitre having taken his celebrated Château Rouge-gorge to shiny new purpose-built premises in the hills) and laid a much-needed car park on the site. In earnest pursuit of the title of *village fleuri*, he had baskets of flowers hung from every lamp post and set up tubs of marigolds, geraniums and lantanas along the main street.

When Marie Claire petitioned him for permission to build a terrace at the side of her café/bar, *l'Estaminet*, M Pardieu graciously consented. No more would her customers have to sip their coffee at minuscule tables on the narrow pavement in front of the café, risking death from diesel fumes and erratic drivers. Papa Pardieu had put the village firmly on the map.

The new mayor had gained his nickname in honour of his six children. How this polyprogeniture had come about was a source of delighted speculation among the regulars at the café: visions of the round, pompous, balding little maire in energetic rumpy pumpy with the cool and elegant Madame Pardieu were almost too delicious to contemplate. And there was more. Not only did "Papa" have a fragrant, fruitful wife: he also had a girlfriend - a *petite amie*!

Incredible though it might seem, everybody – apart, presumably from Madame Pardieu – knew that the mayor was carrying on an enthusiastic liaison with Agnes, Gaston Leblanc's niece, who worked in the *boulangerie* on Thursdays and Saturdays.

To tell the truth, Agnes was a little bit jealous of Joséphine, who, as his secretary, had daily contact with the *maire*, but Agnes needn't have worried. Joséphine had her own *petite amie:* they lived as sisters in her snug little cottage just outside the nearby village of Les Herbes. Suffice it to say they were not related.

Papa Pardieu's latest project had been the renovation of the old *haut-parleurs* (loudspeakers) on the church and *cave cooperative*, and the re-institution of a vocal commentary on village life. In years gone by it had been the *tambour* who roamed the streets of Morbignan with his drum, calling out the news of the day. A previous enlightened and forward-thinking mayor had replaced him with the broadcast commentary, immediately dubbed '*Allo! 'Allo*! because of its way of announcing itself, but the system had lately fallen into disuse.

Naturally, as secretary to the *maire*, it fell to Joséphine to be the new voice of '*Allo! 'Allo*! She took to the job like a duck to the proverbial; indeed, she looked a little like a duck, waddling round the village with her chin held high. Joséphine was, in her own mind at least, a Person of Importance.

All that changed the night of the Great Fire.

It was a Thursday. Joséphine and Marguerite were celebrating their third anniversary that day, and Marguerite had promised to cook a special cassoulet to mark the occasion. Joséphine couldn't wait to get home: at five to six she was busily tidying her desk and checking her handbag for the small gift she had purchased in her lunch hour. Unfortunately for her plans, she had forgotten about JoJo.

JoJo and his pizza van were regular and very welcome Thursday visitors to Morbignan. Connoisseurs of the delicacy claimed his bases were the lightest, his Margaritas and *Fruits de Mer* the most succulent of any pizza to be had in the area. The ladies, from giggling teenagers to sedate matrons, were won over by the twinkle in his dark eyes, the suggestive grin lurking beneath the luxuriant moustache. The moustache, JoJo reckoned, sold just as many pizzas as his culinary skills.

On the fateful Thursday, Joséphine was just about to leave when JoJo put his head round the door.

'*Merde!*' thought Joséphine, plastering on a smile, and reached for the microphone to announce his arrival.

'*Allo! Allo*!' she gabbled. '*Le camion de pizza JoJo est installé sur la place...*' In her haste, she had knocked over the coffee cup on her desk. It only held a few cold dregs, though, and Joséphine reckoned it could wait until morning. She had more important things to think about than a small coffee spill.

At two o'clock the following morning, a giant digger trundled through Morbignan on its way to a construction site north of the village. Its steel treads made short, if noisy, work of the speed bumps, and the nearby houses shivered in sympathy. Wakened villagers cursed the noise and went back to sleep.

In the *mairie*, the little coffee puddle on Joséphine's desk awoke and stretched. It crept along the vibrating desk and curled itself around the microphone switch; finding a tiny gap, it began to explore downwards.

It wasn't the banging on the front door that woke Jeannette, but her dog Useless, who landed on the bed in an urgent, barking heap, frantically paddling with her paws at her sleeping family.

'Useless? What on earth's the matter?' Jeannette peered at the alarm clock. 'It's four in the morning, for heaven's sake.'

'Mmmf? Wossit?' Henry, hr husband, was making a valiant effort to seem awake.

Useless stopped barking long enough for them to hear the insistent knocking below. Jeannette stumbled downstairs, wincing as her bare feet met the stone-flagged kitchen floor. She opened the front door to find her neighbour Alice, in pyjamas and dressing gown, her hair standing on end.

'Fire!' said Alice breathlessly. 'There's fire in the village. Listen.'

Henry appeared at Jeannette's shoulder.

'Whaat…?'

Both women shushed him. All three listened to the hissing crackle: the fire was somewhere close.

'We have to call the *pompiers forestiers*,' said Jeannette. Forest fires were a serious threat at that time of year. After a scorching summer, when the earth was tinder-dry and the *vendange*, the grape harvest, was over, piles of vine stumps, and the thinner, whippy branches known as *sarments* stood at the fields' edges. Soon the villagers would come to help themselves to this flammable bounty for their late barbecues and the aromatic log fires to come.

Two years earlier, Jeannette and Henry had driven out to dinner with some friends in the hills above Morbignan, only to be driven back as flames swept from tree to tree across the road.

The firemen didn't hang about. Within minutes they were racing up the main street in their huge scarlet four-by-four Renault truck, swerving into *the rue de l'église* with a roar that banished sleep. The fire engine had hardly stopped before half a dozen firemen leapt out, braced for the onslaught.

There was nothing. Jeannot, the boss, stood foursquare in his yellow waterproofs, his thumbs hooked in the braces that held up his heavy trousers. He listened intently. Sure enough, the hiss and crackle of the flames could be heard, but where was the smell? No scent of wood smoke drifted through the streets, deliciously reminiscent of summer barbecues, but with deadly implications in the early hours of the morning.

The *pompiers* were diligent. They searched the narrow streets, they sniffed attentively, they paused to listen, trying to gauge the location of the fire. There was nothing. After an hour the firemen gave up; they climbed back into the fire truck and roared off into the dawning day. Sleepers disturbed for the third time that night threw open their shutters and hurled oaths at the departing vehicle.

Morbignan woke to the sounds of a fire where no fire was to be seen. Gaston LeBlanc heard it, firing up his ovens for the morning round of baking. Matthieu the plumber, out on an emergency call, and Didier, on his way to the vines, heard the sizzle and pop. Jules et Jim, in the hills above the village, heard it faintly above the bleating of their goats.

Joséphine, arriving from home, stepped out of her Renault Clio and paused in shock. Fire! Had someone called the *pompiers*? Fumbling with the heavy iron key, she unlocked the door of the mairie. The hiss was even louder in her office: it came from the microphone. *Merde*! She must have left it switched on in her haste to leave yesterday evening. Scarlet-faced, she reached for the switch, but no: it was safely closed.

M. Pardieu arrived in a hurry.

'What's going on?' he barked.

'I don't know, *Monsieur le Maire*. I was afraid I might have left the microphone on last night…' Seeing his frown, she went on hastily, 'but I didn't. Look.'

The mayor peered at the offending mike. He tutted, he said 'Aha' several times in a knowing manner. He stuck his head out of the *mairie* door. Sure enough, the static from the microphone was being faithfully broadcast by the loudspeakers on the church and the *cave cooperative*.

'It's nothing,' he called to the little group who had gathered outside the *mairie*. 'Just a technical hitch. We are dealing with it. Joséphine,' he added, going back inside, 'get on to Languedoc Audio and have them come here *tout de suite*. They installed the system, and they can fix it.'

François arrived from Languedoc Audio red-faced and apologetic. How could anything have gone wrong, he blustered. He had personally seen to the wiring, the installation of the haut-parleurs and the connection of the microphone.

Armed with a voltmeter and wiring pliers he investigated the mike, tapping here, testing there. Muttering wisely to himself, he prised off the top of Joséphine's desk, emerging with a triumphant 'Aha!'

'There!' he said. 'There's your culprit. Nothing to do with me, just as I told you.'

In the cavern beneath Joséphine's desk, the formerly neat coil of wiring was a half-burnt, sticky mass.

'Something must have dripped down through that crack by the mike,' François explained. 'It would eventually have shorted out the wiring. Who spilled coffee on the desk?'

All eyes turned to the mayor's secretary.

It was a chastened Joséphine who crept through the village during the following weeks. The aura of self-importance was gone, her chin was firmly tucked into her collar, and she avoided eye-contact with the grinning villagers. She went without her lunchtime *petit blanc*, knowing that if she ventured into *L'Estaminet* some wag would be sure to cry '*Au feu*!' ('Fire!) and take out his mobile phone in a pantomime of calling the fire brigade.

Joséphine continued to be the voice of '*Allo! 'Allo*!, carrying out her duties efficiently and conscientiously as she had always done. She treated the butcher, the baker, the greengrocer and even JoJo himself with her usual dignified courtesy, proclaiming their wares in measured tones.

But she never ate another pizza.

Havoc at the Holidays

Celia Miles

On my ninety-fifth, having been long duly dutiful, I intend to play Holiday Havoc.

On New Year's all-day PJs day, my wish list/resolutions include sitting next to Elon Musk on his moon trip with a stopover at Mars, a Wyoming bull-riding rodeo win in chaps and bandana, and an apple, cherry, pecan, key lime, and coconut cream pie throughout the first week—as if there's no tomorrow—in case there isn't.

On Valentine's, cloaked in black from witch's hat and catwoman mask to booted pointy toe, I'll feast on Pilgrim-plain unstuffed, half-baked turkey supplemented by Claxton's Fruit Cake and hickory nut coffee. Thirteen white plastic pumpkins and a dozen "Vote for…various losers" signs festoon the lawn.

At Easter I'll frolic in heavy winter wool socks, gloomy hoodie, and fleece-lined jeans, decorating crates of canned cranberry sauce with swaths of wreaths of holly and mistletoe. My red stocking'll adorn the mantel. I'll down several cups of super sweet Noel eggnog alternating with several shots of single malt Scotch, no ice.

Thanksgiving'll be a fasting time—sunup to sundown, twelve empty hours and counting. I'll huddle in a pink bonnet, with purified water, weight-loss pills, and fizzy bubbly Alka-Selzers at hand. In darkness I'll succumb to three brightly colored eggs and fifteen green jelly beans.

Christmas'll find me sulking under a tanning blanket, daring joy to intrude. I'll slather peanut butter on white bread, Velvetta on graham crackers, drink Kool Aid, devour a chocolate bunny. No hopeful lights, family, friends, presents under a no tree—just poor pitiful me.

On my ninety-sixth, maybe I'll return to normal—if I'm lucky.

Fleeting Forever Friend

Ellen Notbohm

"How long do you have to know someone before they're your friend?" my young son wondered, struggling to understand the devilishly nuanced concept of friendship. How would he know if they're a real friend? We had long talks about how friendship can come in all degrees. They can last for years, or they can be brief and situational, but unquestionably genuine. This I learned as a child myself.

Even eight-year-olds dressed up for airplane trips in 1960s. Hence my flying from Oregon to Chicago in a bright white pique dress with a black-and-white checked hem and sash. From my aisle seat at the back of the plane, I could see my parents and little brother several rows ahead. I didn't mind sitting alone. I felt worldly. The stewardess brought breakfast: eggs over easy, toast triangles soaked in margarine, a tiny cup of canned fruit cocktail. My mother despised margarine and fruit cocktail, so I felt even more worldly gobbling them, quite literally, behind her back. The greasy damp bread and slippery grapes would never have been a first choice for breakfast, but opportunities for small acts of defiance rarely came my way. That made them delicious.

However, the egg was trickier. Hard-boiled or scrambled, those were acceptable ways to eat a yolk, but this one ran all over the plate like yellow blood from a paper cut. Revolted, I tried to cut around it delicately, to pop small bites of the whites into my mouth. Even on an airplane, it felt rude to reject the meal, even if politely.

Then, calamity. A splotch of egg yolk, blinding as the sun, landed on my white collar, spreading through the mesh fabric like an inkblot.

I must have gasped in horror, because the man seated next to me glanced over. As I scraped at the stain with my napkin, he said gently, "That will only make it worse."

Indeed, little balls of napkin stuck to the stain, unchanged for my efforts. When my tears brimmed, the man spoke again. "It's just a small stain. I'm sure it will come out. That's such a pretty dress. It doesn't ruin it at all."

"My mother will be angry," I told the nice man, which wasn't true. My mother never angered over small mishaps. I was angry with myself, dribbling food like a two-year-old. I added, "We're going to see my grandparents," doubting whether he could understand how rare and important this was.

"I'm sure they'll be so happy to see you that they won't even notice a tiny spot on your dress."

I finally looked up at this kind man, who had magically said exactly the right thing. Sandy-colored brows topped his light blue eyes, and he wore a black uniform with brass buttons and white braid trim. He said he was Captain Smith, and that he had a daughter about my age.

"She calls me Cap'n Crunch," he told me, making me giggle in spite of myself. "But we still won't buy the cereal." I nodded, no, my mom wouldn't buy it either. She bought things like Cornflakes and Puffed Rice and suddenly I was telling him why I thought Puffed Rice was ridiculous. It just sits there on the milk, bobbing like balloons in a bathtub, until it soaks up enough milk to sink and turn to mush. Captain Smith laughed and said I'd described Puffed Rice perfectly, yes, it was like eating Styrofoam, and thank you, because now he would remember me and never eat it again.

At O'Hare, I introduced Captain Smith to my parents. He told them what a charming daughter they had, and wished them a pleasant time in Chicago.

Hurtling down the expressway in our rental car, my mother remarked, neither kindly or unkindly, that Captain Smith wasn't a real captain, not in the U. S. military, nor an airline pilot. He was a captain in the Salvation Army.

The Christmastime bell-ringers with the coin buckets? How did she know this? Something about his uniform? What was I supposed to do with this information? It made no difference to me. Captain Smith knew just what I needed to hear at the moment I most needed it. He was indeed my salvation. He was my friend. Even if ever so briefly, real enough for me.

***

A few years into a new millennium, *Fly the friendly skies* is now a laughably antique ad slogan. I'm standing in a long line waiting to go through customs, to be questioned by unsmiling fellow American citizens so I can end my research trip and get back to my own country. The line snakes between coils of nylon ropes back and forth, back and forth, ensuring that I'll end my exhilarating adventure in this most boring manner possible.

To pass time, I mentally catalog the crowd ahead of me. One thing's for sure: no one dresses up to fly anymore. They barely dress at all. Women in sandals comprised of a cardboard-thin soles with a pipe-cleaner strips of grimy plastic for straps. Women wearing tops that expose their brassieres. Men displaying several inches of underwear above low-slung pants. Wait, are those pants—or pajama bottoms? Two charmers have skipped the underwear and treat us to an inch of butt crack.

My eyelids grow heavy with tedium.

"Ma'am? Step up, please." A man behind a counter beckons to me, his shirt as white as my long-ago dress. Navy blue and gold epaulettes gleam from the shirt's shoulders; detailed cloth badges garnish the chest and sleeves. He takes my passport and says, "I have to ask you to step out of line and follow me."

His ID tag smacks away any trace of indifference I've been nursing. *It can't be*. But it is.

Cap Smith

Cap Smith might be all of 38 years old, a study in deadpan coolness. He leads me to a female agent. I don't allow myself to wonder anything. My backpack contains nothing remarkable. Laptop, trail mix, book of crossword puzzles. The female agent asks me to step through a metal detector. Nothing unusual there. But then I'm taken to a private side station where she says, "I'm sorry about this. I have to pat you down. Please put your arms over your head." I feel the reluctance in her hands as they move down my body, under my breasts and between my legs. With another "I'm sorry about this," the agent pulls the waistband of my pants out a few inches and peeks down.

Now I balk. "What's going on here?" I ask, in a pointedly reasonable tone. But the agent simply repeats, "I'm sorry about this," and tells me to turn my palms up. "I have to swab you," she explains-apologizes.

"For what?"

"Traces of explosives."

Now I find my full voice. "What reason do you have to think—"

The agent quickly runs a fabric-covered wand over my hands and inserts it into the detection instrument. No lights blink. No alarms sound. She turns and looks me in the eye, a look of empathy and compassion. "None, ma'am. We're randomly testing every 20th person today. It's September 11."

"So someone with explosives on their hands has a 95% change of not getting caught."

What can she say? She has no more voice in these procedures than me.

"I know you're just doing your job," I say, shouldering my backpack. There's a weariness in her smile as she directs me back into the mainstream of the customs area, where the po-faced Cap Smith flicks his eyes from my passport picture to my real mug, then hands my passport back and wordlessly gestures me to a line funneling the random 5% through a door and back into the main concourse. Just another heifer in his cattle drive.

A suppressed snort collides with my sealed lips and shoots up my nose as I hear my son's voice in my head. *Tell it, Mom!* Oh, yes, I'll tell it. How a long ago one-hour friendship has stayed with me a lifetime. I wait until I'm three steps from the door, bolting distance, before I turn back to the implacable Cap and call to him, "I knew Captain Smith. I flew with Captain Smith. Captain Smith was a friend of mine. You, sir, are no Captain Smith."

Sounds of Silence

Steve Putnam

I'm excited about our day at the Psychedelic Supermarket, named after a music venue in Boston, back in the sixties. Today's *Supermarket* is a museum, full of remnants that make you want to celebrate the hip bygones. And mourn, wondering where all the flowers went. Unsure of what I'm thinking, I squirrel a triangulated square of chocolate in my backpack—not to calm my nerves, but to relive a life I've almost forgotten.

The downside, my boss is coming along to reevaluate my performance—an add-on for a Performance Improvement Plan that already recommended me for a cost-cutting, early retirement.

It's a setup. I'm somewhat paranoid about my corporate big brother, a nickel-dime boss watching me troubleshoot a funky Supermarket exhibit called *Acoustic Randomization, and Molecular Migration*, featuring effects without apparent causes. I'm the one who helped Randy the artist set up the electronics. Odds are slim, but I might be troubleshooting a problem that I caused.

The security desk looks like it could be just another one of the Supermarket exhibits. Guard's wearing a Sargent Peppered red dayglo military uniform, an album cover memory too gaudy to celebrate a more genuine past. He runs my temporary ID through a barcode reader; it flashes red and sounds a solitary beep. The facial recognition scanner blinks, even though Randy told me it can't tell a dog from a fire hydrant. The guard silently watches my boss and me open our backpacks for inspection. My supervisor carries a tablet. My laptop's loaded with reloading software for artifactual randomizers and molecular migrators. Randy patiently waits—no surprise; he's an artist, dissatisfied with his own exhibit.

Our mission is more serious than it sounds. Without a plan, we're clueless. We need to be careful. Ethics forbid that we change anything that interferes with artistic intent. One mistake could change the exhibit forever. The burp or fart of a false keystroke could trigger an extra-musical note that needs to be unheard. An electrical surge, a loose connection making and breaking a circuit. Bugged software pushing or pulling rhythm like a defective music box corrupting the time signature of sound. Anything's possible. A random, weak indoor breeze could gently dislodge a tin can from a trash heap, marking an erroneous moment in time.

The Supermarket is a maze. No reward for finding the end, the journey is supposed to be a trip in itself. We pass through a laundromat equipped with round-windowed, front-loading washers. One is repurposed to tumble-clean Barbie Dolls, another dry bricks, and one for giant marshmallows. An adjacent space is filled with radios, tuners, receivers transmitting eerie sounds of static, TV screens and monitors displaying electronic snow. Signal generators, voltmeters, ammeters, oscilloscopes, illuminated dials, and screens, electronic faces electrified, tuned in, and turned on to each other.

We browse a library full of books glued together, forming arches, and ceilings that defy gravity. Spines titled: Mr. Wishing Goes Fishing, The Road, Fahrenheit 451, Tropic of Cancer, Boy Next Door, Sister of the Bride, Candy Cane, Real Heroes for Boys, Black Thumb Mystery. . . I'm grokking the endless possibilities. Boss nudges me. "Let's go," Corporate's not paying us to title read." Must be he's already started my evaluation. The good news, if I can't fix the problem, he's the one who taps dances with excuses if our corporate customer develops some attitude.

We enter a large, cavernous space. "Here it is," Randy says as if I don't know already, "*The Acoustic Randomization, and Molecular Migration.*" He sounds proud of his work, relieved we're here, and confident we can solve the problem. We're looking at a wall, collaged with discarded traffic signs, thirty, forty-mile. speed limits, no passing, one-way, dead-end, no parking, stop. Go Children Slow. Automobilia: AC spark plug, Champion, Packard, Chevrolet. There's a HOT L sign; must be the word 'hotel' missing the 'E'.

The signs on the wall frame a mountainous heap of vintage trash rescued from yesteryear: Quart-size cardboard and metal oil cans, Quaker State, Kendall, Mobil Sunoco, Gulf, Valvoline, Castrol, Torcs Checkered Flag; Campbell Soup, Prince Spaghetti, reds, whites, blues, primary colors of broken American dreams. Not that there's a problem, I'm not one to criticize. But I have to say, "There's not much late-vintage or early modern."

First time I've seen Randy smile today. "I avoid materials that I consider too plastic," he says, proud that his junk comes from solid reputable origins.

With a spontaneous cymbal crash from above, we pause. A symphonic out-of-tune mix of cardboard and metal cans bounces slowly downward, a clunky, percussive bumping and grinding, dampened by the rolling cardboard. "There's the proof," Randy says. Tumbling plastic lacks the acoustic depth of cardboard, aluminum, and tin.

"The conveyor drops the cans onto an elevator that lifts the cans upward, to the top of the pile. "I only take responsibility for things I can control," Randy says. "It's a crapshoot. The cans are free to reposition themselves anywhere on the pile. Some lose their balance and tumble downward again."

For a moment, no sound from above. As luck has it, another can loses its weak grip and succumbs to gravity. "Molecular migration in itself sometimes causes vibration," Randy says. "A subtle change can be enough to unbalance the balanced."

I'm just a technician. Real or unreal, 'molecular migration' sounds funky.

I look upward, hopeful to hear more of the random musical sounds. Randy points toward the different instruments attached to the wall, two stories up. A legless baby grand piano, its missing top exposing its long strings and hammers. A large kick drum is poised on a scaffold suspended from the ceiling. On another scaffold perched on the opposite side of the cavernous space, a tom-tom and ride cymbal. Directly above us, a chandelier of many tiny, gaudy-colored lightbulbs surrounded by chimes. It's important to check it all out. It's important to recognize when something is or isn't happening. The disjointed band instruments remain silent, the stack of oil and soup cans, stable.

You can't see the problem, you can only hear the stillness," Randy says. "No sound, no breeze, no tumbling cans. It defeats the purpose of the conveyor. We need the source of the missing notes, sources of the extra silence."

"I understand the concept of random sound. But why the junk heap," I ask.

"Each can, rolling downward announces the passage of another moment in time. It's not a new idea."

"Then why the music?

"Why not? Random sound mixed with silence creates an acoustic backdrop for the falling riffraff. "Randy shifts his feet and stands at attention. "Time is of the essence," he says. "In more ways than one."

I like Randy but don't know him well enough to say, 'No shit, Sherlock.'

"Give it more time," the boss says. "The first step in troubleshooting, verify the problem."

We wait There's no immediate relief from the boredom of auditory deprivation interspersed with sensory overloads of momentary percussive sound. Seconds seem like minutes; minutes hours, making me wish a tin can would crash downward, announcing another moment in time.

Missing sounds create problems. You can't tell if there's an electromechanical failure, a defective robotic striker, or a corrupt randomizer chip in the computer. Is it a missing musical note or an added moment of silence? Waiting makes my eyes water and stomach tighten. My head swims within itself. The job might take hours. Boss's brow wrinkles. Maybe he's getting edgy, waiting for a glitch that might be a critical clue for fixing the sound randomizer and molecular migrator.

Kick bass makes a singular deep thud. Another lonely note on a ride cymbal. Nothing on the trash pile falls. "Let's move on," my boss says. This could take some time."

"How much do we know about random sounds?" Randy asks, without allowing us enough time to answer. "It could take a nanosecond for the next lone sound or unsound to happen. It could take five minutes." He leads us through a narrow, dark winding hall, and unlocks an IT closet door. A computer stacked on a server turns on an electromagnetic actuator to kick the bass drum pedal, another the snare, the ride and crash cymbals, and chimes. It plays random notes and rests for erratic moments of silence.

A bass note from the piano interrupts the silence. Again, a pause. A soprano striker strikes a brighter piano string. A pause. I shift my legs, waiting. A drum beat but no cymbal crash. Chimes.

A pause. We might have to wait fifteen seconds. But who knows? It might be fifteen minutes. Thankfully, talking distracts me from the peaceful sounds of nothingness. Boss has a question as if he wants to get Randy to rethink his thoughts. "If we're randomizing silence, why worry about some unknown sound that might go missing?"

"The missing sound is no longer random," Randy replies. It's the interaction of random silence and sound that entertains. You can't have one without the other."

We watch the live video feed as we override the software and trigger sounds with the keyboard. We listen through headphones to monitor the emptiness of the unwanted quietude. Who knows which instrument is cheating museum visitors from hearing random sounds gone missing?

Boss reads our checklist. "Bass kick."

I press the '1' key. We're watching the bass drum feed on the video. The pedal actuates. A pleasant thud comes through both headphone channels. From the mountain top, an oil can bounces downward, another welcome sound breaking the silence.

A ride cymbal moment. "Dig it."

"It sounds cool," the boss says. Guaranteed, he's doing one of his customer relation stunts.

I Press the '2' key. Sure enough, a singular short cymbal sound.

"Bass piano."

The '3' key pressed, no problem. The piano vibes us with another bass note.

So it goes, instrument by instrument. Tambourine, snare, tom-tom. Then we shift to CAPS LOCK shifted with numbers 1 through 9. We hear nine different sets of chimes; everything works. Now and then the trashed oil cans fall downward, triggered by our diagnostic false moments in time

We monitor the computer's randomized music that plays out by chance or clumsy design. We watch and listen to see if there's some sound trigger missing. Since we've already started, I'm not sure why the boss insists that we record the occurrence of each sound on a checklist. He hands me his favorite G-2 Pen. Is impersonating a scientist a new customer relations act he learned at charm school?

Bastardized logic or not, we need to discover the whereabouts of the missing note. Or the missing spot where a silent moment replaced it. Is the missing note lost in cyberspace? Or is it still with us here on earth, playing in someone else's band? We might be dealing with a hack. There might be a weak, unhinged electromechanical striker somewhere on the scaffolded sound stage. Intermittent connection from a loose plug? Corroded keyboard micro switch?

I wonder what the boss is thinking or not thinking. How can lost voids or found musical moments affect my evaluation?

Lost in thought, I've missed an instrumental sound or two that might have been significant. I press the 'Enter' key to start over. Boss mumbles something that's muffle-blocked by my headphones. I'm not a great lip reader but it looked like he maybe said, "Jesus Christ! Not again."

Three sets of chimes riff in a row, separated by brief moments of silence. A long pause that feels like forever. My muscles tighten, breathing goes shallow. My mind swims in its depths, almost drowning in nothingness. Three minutes since I last checked, I glance at my watch.

My perception of time is somehow slow dancing with life, intensifying my thirst for sound. What happens if the program goes silent, or plays a spontaneous symphony?

Fifteen minutes of silence. Randy insists the long delay proves there's something wrong. Boss suggests some chimes might be missing, maybe the number four set. "Jesus," he says. We need to think hijacked. Reload the software. Try again.

Randy is the artist who fears nothingness, real or imagined. Randy is a voice of reason. "You never know how long it takes for a sound delay to become a long riff of silence. Is a missing note wasted if the sound file no longer needs it?

***

No idea which sound or long moment of silence is lost or found. Outside of the server room, I feel a little lost sitting on a boardwalk, a useless bus stop for an orange magic bus. Missing its wheels, it will never come or go. I watch Randy's trash elevator, waiting for another turn-on by another falling can. The silence between notes creates a feeling of expanding emptiness. My mind seems to have lost its will to swim within itself. The silence causes mental dehydration, a thirst to hear the next note. Or two. Anything.

I close my eyes to better ignore passersby who grok at me as if I'm part of the *Randomization and Molecular Migration* exhibit.

The bass drum thuds. Two cans, one on either side of the trash heap, roll down onto the conveyor and toward the elevator for an ascent to the summit of the mountainous trash heap. How long is the wait for the next oil can avalanche to mark another moment in time? Silence assures us that the conveyor is safe from overload. Enjoy the serenity.

My unadulterated mind drifts. What's the meaning of an empty Quaker State oil can? Or Kendall, Sweet Life, Del Monte? Am I a victim of analysis paralysis? I kick back, resting my feet on a handrail, looking at the whole thing, wondering what it all means.

Randy's looking upward toward the drums and piano, trying to follow, trying to predict which note comes next from where?

Bass drum kick, a tom-tom beat, then the snare. Payback for a hard day's work; acoustic thirst quenched by fresh sound. Three chime groups ring one after another; I'm too relaxed to say it might have been numbers 2, 5, and 7. The piano plays a soprano note, a new one that I don't recall. Another striker strikes a thin piano string for a tinny sound at the highest octave. A low, throaty, drawn-out growl—piano bass—the pleasant sound of a dog asleep in its dream world, quenching my thirst for sounds and silence.

Too many cans to count or identify during the avalanche downward, celebrating the fresh sound. The conveyor feeds the elevator. The empty cans rise to the top of the heap, ready for the next fall. I feel a hypomanic rush.

The boss, I'd forgotten. He's to my right, incognito, almost undercover, in the shadow of the bus, stowing his tablet.

My eval must be complete. Another moment passes. I close my eyes and smile a smile that won't give up whether I'm asleep or awake.

Station Love

Souad Zakarani

The train screeches to a halt. Few people want to get off here, in the medium-sized hanseatic city that is nowhere near the sea. And of the few passengers who do, most, including myself, do just that: pass through and move on as soon as their connecting train picks them up. I'm already aware of the arrogance of the foreigner in me, knowing that I really know nothing about this region. There are reasons why people live here, reasons they know and I do not.

As I shoulder my rucksack, dragging my suitcase behind me, my gaze is caught by a brightly colored column. Turquoise at the bottom, then a band of yellow stones, turquoise again at the top, and at the top a purple and black striped onion-shaped belly. The uneven mosaics shine as if polished in the sun. What a beautiful thing you can do with a simple station pillar! I'm already feeling a bit more at home here and trudge on towards the lift. It was then that I noticed that the other columns in the station were also so beautifully designed and colorful. Magical! As I enter the station hall, I'm greeted by even more curved lines, golden spheres, colorful columns and floors and walls decorated with colorful mosaics. Lights are falling in from somewhere and reflecting off small mirrored stones around the room. You can't rush past here, you have to stop and look! That's probably the only reason for the long waits between trains.

After spinning around like a stargazer, I want to follow the aroma of coffee. But my suitcase catches on something. I turn and see it, or rather it, the body, a woman's body. She's crouching with her face against the wall, her hands spread out.

"Are you all right?" is my first impulse. But her face, now turned towards me and smiling, doesn't show any discomfort. Quite the opposite. I'm overcome by the uneasy feeling that I've disturbed her in some way.

"Thank you, I'm fine. I was just saying hello to my lover".

A soulful smile in the midst of countless freckles. My questioning look seems to amuse her, then her eyes wander back to the wall. Her delicate fingertips caress the rough white. She says goodbye with a fleeting kiss and whispers a barely audible "see you later".

"Isn't he attractive?" she beams in my direction.

"Who?" I look around, hoping to find the answer myself.

"It is! My station!" she exclaims happily, arms raised.

Contrary to my expectations, her volume doesn't attract any attention. The saleswoman in the bistro a few meters away carries on, arranging the pastries so that, despite the gaps, it looks like there's plenty to choose from. An elderly woman in an apron sweeps invisible dirt from the corners near the exit.

"Oh, this is your station? You really have done a wonderful job! Great design!" Now I too am happy to be able to pass on my enthusiasm directly to someone else. Her warm brown eyes smile:

"No, I didn't design it, that was the famous Mr. Hundertwasser. Just look at all the shapes and colors! And that wall fountain! A dream of a place! Everything is in flow! You would fall in love with it, wouldn't you?

I nod hesitantly, because it really is beautiful here.

"When this magnificent building was inaugurated in November 2000, it was all over for me and my Friedrich." Her eyes sparkle with tears. "I'm going to tell you something, but don't think I'm crazy."

I nod, astonished at such intimacy, and lean towards her.

"We got married two years ago. Friedrich and I. I just felt that he liked me too. I have been coming here every day ever since by train, of course."

I nod once more in understanding, although I do not understand a word. Uncertain, I dare to ask: "Excuse me... and who is Friedrich now?"

"Well, the station," she explains with warm, matter-of-fact sincerity. As if she could see the error of her statement in my look, she continues:

"Of course it's called Friedensreich Hundertwasser Station, but because it's so close and familiar to me, I call it Friedrich. When we're intimate, it's sometimes Fritz too".

When we're intimate ... I seem to have lost the thread forever, and I don't know if I'm interested in finding it again.

"Do you have a family?" she tears me from my thoughts.

"Um, no," I answer for the sake of simplicity, wanting that coffee now more than ever. I nod in the direction of the bistro and leave. She smiles at me understandingly as her right hand runs gently over a mosaic surface.

The coffee is good, hot and strong. It's steaming in front of me in the seating area of the bistro. I enjoy the peace and quiet of being the only customer in this modern living room, with its floral wallpaper, artificial plants and warm bar lighting. My thoughts are still circling around my strange encounter.

When we're intimate ... How can you be intimate with an inanimate object? Various sex toys immediately come to mind. Still, what does this woman get back from the building? Affection? Compliments? Comfort? Hardly. Security and warmth? Maybe. Stability? Sure. She's been abandoned and disappointed by previous partners. Conflict and arguments are certainly out of the question in a building like this. Comfortable one-way communication? I stare into my now empty coffee cup, as if the answers lie somewhere at the bottom.

"Would you like anything else?" the salesperson behind the counter asks kindly. I reply with a question of my own:

"Tell me, that woman in the station hall; is she really here every day?"

"Well, whenever I work here, I see her. Only once was she absent for two days. When she came back, she asked me if something had happened; she'd been ill and couldn't come".

I am surprised that she doesn't judge the woman at all. I was almost expecting a slanderous tone, and now I am ashamed.

"Why do you think this woman comes here so often?" I ask.

"She told me she was more comfortable here than at home. Well, she always looks so happy... I like working here too, but I also like going home at night." Still no disparagement in her voice, just a wink at her last words.

"So nobody cares about her or what she does?"

A shrug. "She doesn't hurt anyone. Sometimes she even shops here and we exchange a few pleasantries." Her eyes search and find the woman, who is now sitting by the wall fountain with a dreamy expression on her face. "I actually like her."

After clearing her plate, she wishes me a good journey and disappears behind the counter. Our conversation seemed over.

Three weeks later, my return journey takes me back to the Hundertwasser station. Once again, I had to wait - this time for a full ninety minutes. It's an unpleasantly long delay, but after my stay at the spa by the sea, nothing throws me off balance so easily. Thanks to meditation, craft evenings and walks. I greet the colorful mosaic columns on the platform almost like old friends. It feels so warm and familiar that I even briefly consider just leaving my luggage on the platform. But when I realize that I'll probably be the only person whose luggage has been stolen from this place in a hundred years, I abandon the idea. This time I take the spiral staircase to have a closer look at the wall fountain. As the lift is out of order, the other eleven people who have got off also want to take the stairs - unlike me, they are in a hurry. Silently, clearly annoyed, they push past me, threateningly shaking my rucksack, suitcase and three extra bags of souvenirs and handicrafts. They're probably here more often than I am, and no longer have an eye for art. Maybe they never did. My path leads me back to the bakery bistro, where I have to share the living-room atmosphere with a family of five and an elderly couple.

They all communicate very loudly for various reasons, so I inevitably eat and drink faster and soon find myself back in the station hall. I briefly consider exploring the town, but with my poor sense of direction, I wouldn't be able to find my way back in time for the departure. Instead, I shuffle into the small souvenir shop next door. Scarves, ceramics, soaps, jewelers - everything can be sold as Hundert Wasser art. There are also postcards and books on display. I browse a bit, reading here and there. I also read about Hundert Wasser's aversion to straight lines, which is evident everywhere in this building and makes him attractive to me.

"So, are you back?"

I turn and look into reddened eyes.

"Have you seen it yet? I don't understand how this graffiti can make anyone happy!" She points to a black train of graffiti in the station concourse.

"Oh," I search for comforting words, "I'm really sorry about your... well, about the beautiful building." But she only seems more upset.

"I hope they clean it up soon!" I try to console her again. But my experience tells me that unwanted graffiti tends to stay.

The woman doesn't seem convinced either. "Maybe I'll just paint over it myself. That can't be against the law..." Her desperation made me uncomfortable. In my helplessness, I randomly grab an art card and put it next to the cash register.

"That's thirty." - Such an embarrassingly cheap way out that I quickly slip away with a "All the best".

So object love is not all that stable, I think to myself as I get back on the train. One can just come along and hurt the other. Whether it's a person or an object, we never seem to be able to protect our loved ones completely. I think of my neighbor who, years after her death from cancer, still mourns his wife. Or my father who, despite all our love, was crushed by the bullying of his superiors. What is certain?

I look at the art on my card for a while. I hear the train arriving in the distance and feel a tender connection with this woman who loves this little piece of earth with all her heart.

We Are…

Mike Turner

We're the ocean in a droplet
A breath in deep blue skies
A whisper in the murmuring wind
The love in a child's eyes
A light in deepest darkness
Contentment in a sigh
We're the promise of all tomorrows
Each moment
For all time

Geraniums

Nancy Dillingham

And geraniums in the window. Red ones.
—Marilynne Robinson

He remembers well
seeing her just-washed hair—

prematurely white—
down for the first time

spread over her shoulders
like angels' wings

the surprise in her green eyes
her sweeping black lashes

the bittersweet smell of geraniums
wafting through the open window

when he kissed her—
just once—

on her mouth
before everything went south

Still a blooming heart is stout
with roots that never give out

A Midwinter Night's Dream

Patricia Feinberg Stoner

Christmas Eve. In the little French village of Morbignan la Crèbe, Martha Patterson was checking lists.

Goose—yes: her husband Richard was on his way to collect the splendid bird ordered from the butcher in Bédarieux. Sprouts, carrots, chestnuts, potatoes for roasting, all prepared and waiting in the fridge. The pudding—Martha prided herself on her home-made Christmas puds—was sitting in the larder, gently reeking of cognac and awaiting its second boiling on Christmas morning. More cognac fumes wafted from the generous bowl of brandy butter in the fridge.

For those with stout appetites there would be mince pies and Christmas cake for later. Although fully integrated into their adopted French home, Martha and Richard Patterson liked to do Christmas the English way.

Martha was looking forward to tomorrow's organised chaos. She and Richard would enjoy a quiet exchange of presents, then the traditional breakfast: smoked salmon, scrambled eggs and a glass of buck's fizz to fortify them against the onslaught to come.

Of the invited guests, Marie Claire and Gaston would arrive early, with Gaston's daughter Jeannette and her husband Henry in tow, plus their toddler Marie Bernadette and their dog Useless. Bang on time would come James and Alex Carcenet, accompanied by Alex's indomitable mother Betty. Bernard Durand and his wife Lili would make up the party.

Sure as eggs were little green apples, another knock on the door would come. One, or several, of the neighbours would drop in to wish them *Joyeux Noël*, and gaze wistfully at the happy group round the log fire, until invited to join them for a glass of pastis or, for the more adventurous, mulled wine. Eventually, as all the uninvited guests were shooed gently out of the door, the feast would begin.

A stamp of boots in the porch roused Martha from her musings.

'That you, love?' she called, as Richard made his way into the room, shrugging off his heavy overcoat. He was, she noticed, carrying a large brown paper bag; there seemed to be something moving inside it.

'Oooh! Presents?' Martha exclaimed, making a beeline for the bag.

'No,' said her husband, looking slightly bewildered. 'I found this on the doorstep. It isn't addressed to either of us. In fact, it isn't addressed at all.'

'Well then, let's see what's to do.' Martha plunged her hand into the bag, then jumped back with a yelp. 'Something bit me!' she said, sucking her finger. 'You haven't gone and got a puppy, have you?'

'Of course not,' said Richard indignantly. 'You know Visitor prefers to be an Only Dog. Let's see what it is.'

Patterson turned the bag upside down and shook it gently. With a most un-Christmaslike oath a very small person tumbled out. He was dressed in a green suit with green and white striped stockings and a tall green woolly hat with a bobble on it.

'Who on earth are you, where did you come from and what are you doing in my kitchen?' Patterson wanted to know. Martha was quicker on the uptake.

'I know!' she said. 'You must be one of Santa's Little Helpers.'

The small person glared at her.

‘That job description is not only obsolete, it is demeaning. I am the Senior Assistant to the Deputy Chief Vice President (Seasonal Operations). You may call me Galadriel.’

‘*Galadriel?*’ Martha and Richard exclaimed in unison.

‘What can I tell you? My mother was a *Lord of the Rings* fan.’

‘But,’ Martha began, wondering how to put this tactfully, ‘wasn’t Galadriel, er, female?’

‘Dear, dear, you really are behind the times,’ said the elf crossly. ‘Such outmoded gender stereotypes have no place in this century. My pronouns, by the way, are itsElf and itsElfin.’

‘Yes, but why are you here? And how did you get here?’ said Martha.

‘Well, that’s quite a story,' said the elf. ‘I saw a brown paper bag on Santa’s table and I thought it might be my pizza from Deliveroo Gnome Service. I was hungry, so I climbed inside, but it only had a crummy old PlayStation in it. I was about to climb out again when *someone* (I name no names) grabbed the sack. I was whisked through the air and dumped into the sleigh before I could shout for help.’

‘I don’t wish to be rude,’ Richard Patterson butted in, ‘but how are you planning to get back?’

‘Back? I should coco. It’s cold up there, and there’s nothing to see but white outside, and a lot of stupid elves inside. Oh, and Santa’s great fat bum as he fiddles with…’

Here Martha gasped.

‘… his sleigh.’ The elf concluded, with a reproving look in her direction. ‘You’ve got a lovely fire going, and a great big sparkly tree. Might there be a present under it for me?’

‘There might *not*,’ said Richard firmly. ‘You and your boss are supposed to deliver presents, not get them.’

The elf’s shoulders slumped. His lower lip came out.

‘There, there,’ said Martha. ‘It is Christmas, after all. You can stay for a glass of mulled wine, but you must be gone before our guests get here. They wouldn’t understand.’

As if summoned by the words “mulled wine,” a peremptory knock was heard at the front door. Martha glanced at her watch with a worried expression. Now was not a time to entertain more guests. Her husband, meanwhile, was ushering in a tall, distinguished (if somewhat rotund) gentleman in impeccable evening dress. His white beard was groomed to perfection and his eyes twinkled with appropriate merriment.

‘I do hope I’m not intruding,’ said this apparition, ‘but I believe you have a young employee of mine here.’ His English was flawless, yet was there just a hint of something—perhaps Scandinavian?—in his accent.

The elf was doing his best to hide behind Visitor and the two cats on the hearth. Banjax swatted him away with a sleepy paw.

‘I’m not here’ he mouthed frantically at Martha, who ignored him.

‘A young employee?’ said Richard Patterson. ‘If you are who I think you must be…’ the stranger bowed in acknowledgment ‘… then shouldn’t you be wearing a red suit and long black boots?’

‘Good gracious, dear boy,’ said Santa—for indeed it was he. ‘You don’t think I’d come calling in my work clothes? That would be most frightfully rude.’

‘Well, this will take some explaining,’ said Martha. ‘Come and sit by the fire and have a drink, and we can sort it all out.’

‘You brought me here, boss,’ said the elf. ‘You swept me up in that paper bag, and before I had time to say “Oi!” you’d dumped me in the sleigh, and the next thing I knew I was on these good people’s doorstep. And I have to say it’s a lot nicer here than up North.’

‘Why, what’s wrong with up North?’ Santa looked concerned. ‘Don’t we treat you properly? Meal breaks and time and a half for Sundays and so forth?’

'Yes, that's all very well, but it's boring up there. And it's hard work too, all that stuffing X-boxes and Furbys into sacks, and the endless trudging back and forth, back and forth to Amazon since they've refused to deliver to the north pole. And the cold, don't get me started on the cold…'

'It does sound a little harsh,' said Martha sympathetically.

'Yes, perhaps, but it's only for a couple of months. And then there's the long summer holiday to look forward to.'

'I didn't know they get a holiday,' Richard said.

'Of course they do! This isn't the dark ages. But I'd forgotten our friend here is very young—he only joined the team this year. He probably doesn't know he gets a holiday. I'll bet he signed his contract without reading it—they all do.'

Richard had a faraway look in his eyes that Martha knew all too well. 'Now I wonder,' he mused, 'where Santa and the Elves go for their vacation?'

'Mrs Claus and I prefer a quiet time in Europe, now we're getting on a bit: we've got a nice little villa in Tuscany. But for the elves we always arrange a trip to somewhere warm. This year I believe they're going to the Seychelles.'

'The Seychelles?' the elf pricked up his ears. 'I've always wanted to go there.'

'So, what's it to be? Are you staying here with these good folk, or are you coming back to the north pole with me?'

'Hang on, guv, I'll get my hat!'

Half an hour later Richard and Martha were sitting by the fire, a cat on each lap and Visitor asleep on Richard's feet, discussing their strange encounter.

'That's one story we can never tell,' Martha said. 'Nobody would believe us. They'd think we'd taken leave of our senses.'

'You're right,' her husband agreed, 'it's a *story* we can never tell. On the other hand…'

Martha smiled to herself. Soon her husband the poet would be reaching for his notebook.

'I've got an idea for the poem,' she said. 'Why not call it *A Midwinter Night's Dream*?'

She leaned forward in her chair. Richard did the same. Solemnly they high-fived.

The Last Straw

Saeed Ibrahim

The rich musical tones of the antique doorbell sounded once more in Prema Ramaswamy's drawing room as one more member arrived at her Book Club morning. Prema's thirty year old book club was one of Bangalore's oldest and most sought after book clubs with a select membership of well informed and well-to-do society women. The group met once a month in Prema's spacious and stylish home in Richmond Town, one of the few surviving remnants of the old colonial-style bungalows. With the city's fast changing architectural landscape her residence stood out prominently with its imposing front porch, stunning Tuscan pillars and unmistakable 'monkey tops' - pointed canopies covering a Mangalore tiled sloping roof.

The women present were getting a bit impatient as they waited for the two absent members to show up before the start of the proceedings.

"I don't think either of them is coming today," offered Mrs. Menon. "It's no use waiting for them anymore."

"Don't tell me they have had another quarrel and don't want to face each other or be seen together," queried Mrs. Deshmukh with a knowing smile.

"Don't you know? That is precisely what has happened. I have all the details from Mrs. Coutinho," piped in Mrs. Singh smugly with the air of someone who is privy to information that is not known to others.

The assembled ladies turned to her with renewed interest as she continued, "Mrs. Coutinho was away for two weeks on a holiday in Europe and she left her plants in Mrs. Chatterjee's care to be watered and taken care of in her absence. It seems that on her return, Mrs. Coutinho found that all her plants had died and she is totally upset with Mrs. Chatterjee for her carelessness. Quite obviously the two are not talking to each other." There was an audible sigh of resignation from the gathering and the book club meeting got underway.

Mrs. Alice Coutinho and her friend Mrs. Sonali Chatterjee had been neighbours for as long as they could remember and whilst their friendship had blossomed and flourished over the years, it had not been without its ups and downs, and its blow hot blow cold moments. Many in their circle of friends marvelled at the closeness they shared but wondered at the love-hate nature of their relationship as they fell out with each other at regular intervals, but then predictably made up again soon after.

During episodes when they were apparently not on talking terms, the two ladies passed the word around amongst their mutual friends about the reason for their discord and each presented her side of the story. But their friends knew better than to take sides, for they were confident that sooner or later the thaw would set in and it would once again be business as usual. The fact was that their mutual dependence made it impossible for the two women to be at war with each other for too long, and yet their vastly differing natures made their periodic rows part and parcel of their existence.

Alice was a spare and sprightly woman in remarkably good shape for her 70 years. Having been a captain in the national women's hockey team, she continued to exercise regularly and never used the lift to go up and down the stairs to her third floor apartment. She was meticulous in her habits and led a Spartan lifestyle, having stoically adjusted to her single status after losing her husband twenty years earlier. She was frank and outspoken and expressed her views freely about people whose habits she disliked or issues that she did not see eye to eye with. Often, she would openly criticise even her close friends in front of others making the latter feel uncomfortable and wondering what she said of them when they were not around. Wary of her caustic tongue, people had come to realise that it did not pay to get on her wrong side.

Alice's neighbour Sonali, at 55, was a much younger woman, laid back and with an artistic temperament, dreamy and forgetful;

some even called her slightly wacky. She dabbled in oil paintings which were at times quite impressive and gained her a lot of profit and praise at the annual art exhibition that she held at a local gallery. Her husband, a scholar and visiting professor, adored her, rarely got in her way when he was around (which was not often), and allowed her plenty of space.

Despite their different temperaments, a certain bond had been created between the two women and they found comfort in the fact that they were there for each other when the occasion demanded. Alice would cat sit for Sonali when she and her husband were away and she also helped keep the accounts for the money earned from Sonali's painting exhibitions. Sonali, for her part, was not herself fond of cooking but hired a cook who served up fairly decent meals. She knew that living on her own, Alice survived on snack type meals and she would often send up a particularly well prepared dish or one that she knew was one of Alice's favourites. Sonali also accompanied Alice for her annual medical check-ups and Alice had given Sonali a spare key to her apartment to be used in case of an emergency.

Apart from these mutually beneficial arrangements, the odd spat occurred from time to time such as when Alice hadn't shown up for one of Sonali's painting exhibitions and Sonali had felt slighted; or when Sonali had, without checking with Alice, allowed a friend to borrow one of Alice's precious coffee table books and the book was never returned.

After the last incident of Alice's withered plants, harmony and peace had somehow returned. Alice had obviously forgiven Sonali because the following month Sonali received a phone call from Alice.

"Hello Sonali, this is Alice. You know it is my birthday next Saturday and I am having a few friends over for cocktails. Please do come and join us. 7:30 should be fine."

Sonali was overjoyed at the apparent patch up, "Thank you, Alice. Of course, I will be there. Is there anything you would like me to bring along?"

"There's nothing I need, Sonali. I have ordered everything from our usual caterer. Maybe you can just come and help me with the flower arrangements."

Sonali arrived early, and with her usual flair decorated Alice's living room with charming little arrangements from the flowers that Alice had ordered. The party was a grand success. Alice had made sure that there was a plentiful supply of wine and spirits and she had ordered a range of delicious snacks and short eats from a catering service she used occasionally. One of Alice's friends had brought along a birthday cake and they all stood in a circle around her singing "Happy Birthday" as she tried to blow out the solitary candle stuck in the middle of her birthday cake. Despite several attempts the trick candle just wouldn't get blown out.

Everyone was in a jolly mood and there was much laughter and leg pulling all around. Vast quantities of wine and liquor were consumed and the snacks ordered by Alice were relished and quickly disappeared. Sonali was the last to leave. It was late at night when, tipsy and feeling quite happy with the world at large, she staggered back to her own home and passed out on her living room sofa.

She woke up the following morning with a massive hangover. Still a bit disoriented, she reached out, as per her habit, for her smartphone to check her messages. She groped all around her but her phone was nowhere to be found. In vain she searched high and low and looked all over the house, her mobile was not there. She had almost given up on ever finding it again, when like a flash it struck her that maybe she had left her phone the previous evening in Alice's kitchen whilst helping to refill the snacks and short eats. However, in her dishevelled state she was feeling too embarrassed to go and ask Alice for her phone. The cobwebs seemed to clear as a brilliant plan formed in her mind. She knew that Alice always took an afternoon nap soon after her lunch, and she was going to use that to her advantage.

She quickly went up to the inner drawer of her cupboard and pulled out the spare key to Alice's flat. Without bothering to check her appearance in the hallway mirror, she quickly ran up unannounced to her friend's apartment, turned the key in the lock as noiselessly as possible and stealthily let herself in. A quick dash into the kitchen and she would regain possession of her precious telephone and exit the apartment without detection. Or so she thought.

Sonali's luck ran out that afternoon. Alice for some reason had not been able to sleep, and she sat up reading in her rocking chair in her bedroom. She thought she heard a sound coming from the main door and felt the presence of someone walking towards her kitchen. She got up and went out to investigate, and let out a horrified scream as she saw Sonali retreating towards the front door clutching something in her hand.

Sonali had been caught red handed. She tried in vain to offer apologies and excuses, but Alice was in no mood to hear her explanations. For Alice this was the last straw and a permanent rupture loomed threateningly ahead. The minor disagreements that they had had in the past were nothing compared to this. A burglar type break-in, a flagrant invasion of her privacy, and a breach of her confidence and trust was something that Alice could neither stomach nor forgive. Her mind was made up. Things could never be the same again between them.

She, however, decided to remain calm and collected. Instead of confronting or remonstrating with Sonali, she decided on a non-combative approach. After a sheepish Sonali had left, Alice with a note of finality picked up her phone, called the locksmith and had him change the front door locks.

Illustrations by Indo-French artist, Danesh Bharucha

About the Authors

Rickie Zayne Ashby is the author of three books. He is retired and lives near bowling green, Kentucky.

Hubert Blair Bonds, a native of Kannapolis, NC, has lived in Atlanta, GA for more than 30 years. He is retired from the federal government with 34 years of service. Currently serving as Curator at the East Point Historical Society, his hobbies include gardening, film history, and writing.

Jim Cherry grew up in Chicago in the 60's, although he missed all the cool things. He's lived in Los Angeles, visited New Orleans, Mexico, France and Germany, usually when he didn't have the money. He's the author of several self-published novels including *Becoming Angel, The Last Stage*, two books of short stories, *Stranger Souls*, and *The Lion Communique*. If you want to know more about Jim, you'll find him in between the lines of his stories.

Janet Clare's first novel, *Time Is the Longest Distance*, was published in 2018 and she previously published fiction and essays in a variety of online journals and anthologies. *True Home* her second novel, will be published May 20, 2025. She lives in Los Angeles.

Jeff Clemmons is a cofounder of M'ville, an Atlanta-based writing salon. In addition to writing two books – *Rich's: A Southern Institution* and *Atlanta's Historic Westview Cemetery* – and a screenplay, he, along with three others, was nominated for an Emmy Award for producing Georgia Public Television's "Rich's Remembered." He is currently working on a biography of avant-garde novelist Frances Newman.

Mike Coleman is the author of *The Way from Me to Us: A Memoir* and is a 2024 Georgia Author of the Year Award Finalist. He was recognized in 2025 as an outstanding Georgia author by the Georgia State House of Representatives. Retired after a 45-year writing career spanning journalism, advertising and corporate communications, Coleman lives with his husband, Ted, in Atlanta. In 2027, they will celebrate 50 years together.

Nancy Dillingham is coeditor of four anthologies of western North Carolina women writers. Her poetry collection Home was nominated for a SIBA. Her latest publications are the chapbooks *Promise, Longing*, and *After Helene* and *No Time Like the Present: A Memoir in Essays*, and *Curves: Collected Stories*. She lives in Asheville, NC.

Don Edwards lives and writes in Los Angeles. He is a founding member of True Gospel Bookstore which records his poems as songs.

Martha Ellen lives alone in an old Victorian house on a hill on the Oregon coast. Retired social worker. MFA. Poems and prose published in various journals and online forums including *RAIN, North Coast Squid* and many others. She writes to process the events of her wild life.

Beverly Fisher is a retired attorney living in Clarksville, TN. She is the author of "Grace Among the Leavings"(Thorncraft Publishing 2013).

Ken Gosse usually writes metric, rhymed verse with whimsy and humor. First published in *First Literary Review–East* in November 2016, since then in *Lothlorien Poetry Journal, Pure Slush, Home Planet News Online, WELL READ Magazine*, and others. Raised in the Chicago suburbs, now retired, he and his wife have lived in Mesa, AZ, over twenty-five years with rescue cats and dogs underfoot.

J. B. Hogan has been published in a number of journals including the *Blue Lake Review, Crack the Spine, Copperfield Review, Lothlorien Poetry Journal*, *WELL READ Magazine*, and *Aphelion.* His eleven books include *Bar Harbor, Mexican Skies, Living Behind Time, Losing Cotton*, and *The Apostate.* On June 14, he will be the 2025 inductee into the Arkansas Writers Hall of Fame. He lives in Fayetteville, Arkansas.

Saeed Ibrahim was educated at St. Mary's High School and St. Xavier's College in Mumbai, and later, at the University of the Sorbonne in Paris. He is the author of two books - "Twin Tales from Kutcch," a family saga set in Colonial India, and a short story collection entitled "The Missing Tile and Other Stories." His short stories have appeared in "The Blue Lotus Magazine," "Borderless Journal," "The Hooghly Review," "Different Truths" "Lothlorien Poetry Journal" "WELL READ Magazine" and elsewhere. His other writings include newspaper articles, travel writing, book reviews and two essays for the Museum of Material Memory. Both his books are available on Amazon platforms worldwide.

Michael Lee Johnson is a poet of high acclaim, with his work published in 46 countries or republics. He is also a song lyricist with several published poetry books. His talent has been recognized with 7 Pushcart Prize nominations and 7 Best of the Net nominations. He has over 653 published poems. His 336-plus YouTube poetry videos are a testament to his skill and dedication. He is a proud member of the Illinois State Poetry Society, http://www.illinoispoets.org/, and the Academy of American Poets, https://poets.org/. His poems have been translated into several foreign languages. Awards/Contests: International Award of Excellence "Citta' Del Galateo-Antonio De Ferrariis" XI Edition 2024 Milan, Italy-Poetry. Poem, Michael Lee Johnson, "If I Were Young Again."

Born and reared in Northern Ireland during The Troubles, Colette Lynch's fiction deals with familial crisis and psychological journeys. She has been writing for three years with work published in

The Berlin Literary Review, Litbreak Magazine 2024, and *The Anansi Anthology 2025.*

Fhen M. often returns to the Pagsubay journals edited by David Genotiva, finding particular resonance in Edith Tiempo's entry "Resounding Contemporary Poetic Articulation." A specific line from Tiempo's writing deeply resonates with him: her assertion that "the image being posited against the statement is really saying that the basis of poetry is metaphor." This notion seems to strike a chord with Fhen M., as he frequently revisits and reflects on its significance.

Maria Mackas is a writer, corporate journalist, and professor. She has a Bachelor of Arts in Journalism from the University of Georgia and a PhD in English – Literary Studies from Georgia State University. Born and raised in Atlanta, she lives in Atlanta with her husband, Randy Evans. Her children's book, *Marra's Star*, was published in 2025.

LaVern Spencer McCarthy has published twelve books of short stories and poetry and two journals. She has won over five hundred state awards for her poetry and thirty-four national awards. She is a life member of Poetry Society of Texas She resides in Blair Oklahoma.

Celia Miles, a retired community college instructor, is the author of twelve novels (romance, cozy mystery, historical fiction, maybe "literary,") and co-editor of four women writers' anthologies. Her latest novel is *Eight Nights at the Harris Hotel*, set in the Outer Hebrides.

Karen Miller has worked as a lifestyle writer for 40 years. Her essays and articles have appeared in *The Register-Citizen*, (CT) *The Keene Sentinel*, (NH) the *Marco Island Eagle*, (FL) *Georgia Magazine*, (GA) *Amelia Islander Magazine*, (FL) *Jacksonville Magazine*, (FL) and others. Her book of essays, *Succotash Dreams*, was published in 2013. Her zine, *Grey*, can be found in the Jacksonville Public Library's Zine Collection. She has worked as a blogger, podcaster, cookbook editor, newspaper columnist, and graphic designer. She and her husband have spent the last eight years traveling full time in their van, writing about their adventures on social media. They are currently building an off-grid home in Colorado.

Robin Prince Monroe delights in writing for children; and has authored seven picture books, a middle grade novel, and a chapter book. Recently released titles for grownups include, *Ridiculously Easy Crockpot Recipes, Ridiculously Easy Creative Problem Solving, Time Trees and Grandpa's Knees*, and *Loss of a Loved One*. Her work has also appeared in *Guideposts*, and *Money Matters*. www.RobinPrinceMonroe.com

Mike Nemeth, a Vietnam veteran and former high-tech executive, writes love stories tucked inside murder mysteries. *The Undiscovered Country, Parker's Choice*, and *A Tissue of Lies* are multiple award winners. Mike's works have appeared in *The New York Times, Georgia Magazine, Augusta Magazine, Southern Writers' Magazine*, and *Deep South Magazine. Creative Loafing* named him Atlanta's Best Local Author for 2018.

Ellen Notbohm's work touches millions in more than twenty-five languages. She is author of the award-winning novel *The River by Starlight*, the nonfiction classic *Ten Things Every Child with Autism Wishes You Knew*, and short works appearing in literary journals, magazines, and anthologies in the US and abroad. Her books and short prose have won more than 40 awards worldwide.

Janet Oakley, writing as JL Oakley, writes award-winning historical fiction that spans the mid-19th century to WW II. Her characters, who come from all walks of life, stand up for something in their own time and place: the Pacific NW and WWII in Norway. Though she has lived in the Pacific NW for many years, she has also lived in Hawaii, Washington DC, and Pittsburgh, PA. She has been a guide at Mission Houses in Honolulu, a museum educator at a small NW county museum, and a Humanities Washington speaker on the Civilian Conservation Corps.

Having worked in conflict zones such as Iraq, the West Bank, and Ukraine, Alex Poppe writes about fierce and funny women rebuilding their lives in the wake of violence. She is the award-winning author of four works of literary fiction and *Breakfast Wine*, her memoir-in-essay about her near decade living and working in northern Iraq.

Steve Putnam's short fiction has appeared in *WELL READ Magazine, Main Street Rag, Whiskey Island Magazine*, and Scribes Valley Publishing anthologies. His novel, *Academy of Reality*, a 2019 Faulkner-Wisdom Competition finalist in New Orleans, was recently released by Madville Publishing.

Linda C. Rehkopf is an award-winning author of two books and multiple magazine articles. She writes about life with her dogs from her home in Powder Springs, Georgia, where she lives with her husband and three Labrador retrievers. "Nursery Road," won the Rick Bragg Prize for Nonfiction from the Atlanta Writers Club.

Mike Ross, has flipped burgers at Burger Chef, been a County Jail administrator, a German teacher for 35 years, and a tour guide for 45 years. He lives in Michigan, with his wife, Dianna (an awesome editor), and has loads of kids and grandkids. He is a traveler, runner and skier but his first love is writing.

Cindy Sams is an award-winning journalist and creative nonfiction writer based in Georgia. She holds an MFA in Creative Writing from Reinhardt University and has received honors from the Georgia Press Association. Her hybrid and narrative memoir work has appeared or is forthcoming in *Blue Mountain Review, Plentitudes Journal, The New Southern Fugitives,* and others. Her current project, *Reverse Migration*, blends traditional and experimental forms to trace a Southern girlhood shaped by upheaval, hunger, and fierce resilience. With an ear for dialogue and a sharp eye for contradiction, she writes stories that dig into the cultural and emotional soil of family, memory, and reinvention.

Patricia Feinberg Stoner is an award-winning British writer, a former journalist, copywriter and publicist. She is the author of three humorous books set in the Languedoc, in the south of France - *At Home in the Pays d'Oc, Tales from the Pays d'Oc* and *Murder in the Pays d'Oc* - and also three books of comic verse. Her latest book is a collection of stories about the redoubtable Mrs Arbuthnot, now available from Amazon. You can find her on Facebook on her author's page - Paw Prints in the Butter – and in the writers' group Arun Scribes.

Mike Turner, a poet/songwriter living on the U.S. Gulf Coast, was named 2025 Poet of the Year by the Alabama State Poetry Society. He has more than 475 poems published in over 100 curated literary journals/sites and anthologies; his original songs, recorded both by himself and other vocal artists, are streaming on Spotify, iTunes and YouTube. Mike's poetry collection, Visions and Memories, is available on Amazon.

Micah Ward writes, runs, and enjoys craft beer in middle Tennessee. His short stories have been published in *Well Read* and in anthologies produced by the Colorado Springs Fiction Writers and the Amelia Island Writers clubs. Micah has received three Honorable Mentions from the Lorian Hemingway Short Story Competition and has been nominated for a Pushcart Prize. He was also named Outstanding Club Writer of the year by the Road Runners Club of America for his articles on running.

John M. Williams is a mentor in the Reinhardt University MFA Creative Writing program. He was named Georgia Author of the Year for First Novel in 2002 for Lake Moon (Mercer UP). He has written and co-written numerous plays, with several local productions, and published a variety of stories, essays, and reviews through the years. His and co-author Rheta Grimsley Johnson's play *Hiram: Becoming Hank*, about the formative years of singer Hank Williams, has enjoyed several productions. His most recent books are *Village People: Sketches of Auburn* (Solomon and George 2016), and *Atlanta Pop in the 50s, 60s, and 70s: The Magic of Bill Lowery* (with Andy Lee White) (The History Press 2019), *Monroeville and the Stage Production of "To Kill a Mockingbird"* (The History Press 2023), and his just-released novel *End Times* (Sartoris Literary Group 2023). Other publications can be found on his website at johnmwilliams.net, which hosts his blog, johnmwilliams.net/blog. He lives in LaGrange, Georgia.

Souad Zakarani is a poet, writer and Literature-translator from Morocco. Her works have appeared in many Anthologies worldwide. Her poems, short stories, essays and articles can be read in a variety of international publications, including *WELL READ Magazine, Hooligan Street Poetry, Revista Sofón, RESEARCH PLANET Journal*, and others. In 2025, her poem "Weiß" is shortlisted for Ulrich Grasnik Lyrikpreis.

About the artist

Malcolm Glass has published fifteen books of poetry and non-fiction. His work has appeared in many journals, including "Poetry," "The Sewanee Review," and "The Write Launch." In 2018, Finishing Line Press published his chapbook Mirrors, Myths, and Dreams; and next year Finishing Line will release his triple-hybrid collection, *Her Infinite Variety*.

Also an artist and photographer, Glass has had artwork juried into dozens of exhibitions and galleries, including The Hilliard Gallery, Art Fluent, Photo Artfolio, and Nuu Contemporary Art. His work has won dozens of awards, from honorable mention to Best of Show.

www.ingramcontent.com/pod-product-compliance
Lightning Source LLC
LaVergne TN
LVHW090601110826
845146LV00001B/210

9798989895274